A
CHRISTMAS
ENGAGEMENT

A CHRISTMAS ENGAGEMENT

An Amish Romance

LINDA BYLER

Good Books

New York, New York

The characters and events in this book are the creation of the author, and any resemblance to actual persons or events is coincidental.

A CHRISTMAS ENGAGEMENT

Good Books books may be purchased in bulk at special discounts for sales promotion, corporate gifts, fund-raising, or educational purposes. Special editions can also be created to specifications. For details, contact the Special Sales Department, Good Books, 307 West 36th Street, 11th Floor, New York, NY 10018 or info@skyhorsepublishing.com.

Good Books is an imprint of Skyhorse Publishing, Inc.®, a Delaware corporation.

Visit our website at www.goodbooks.com.

10 9 8 7 6 5 4 3 2 1

Library of Congress Cataloging-in-Publication Data is available on file.

Print ISBN: 978-1-68099-621-0
eBook ISBN: 978-1-68099-682-1

Cover design by Koechel Peterson & Associates

Printed in the United States of America

Chapter One

HER NAME WAS ELIZABETH, BUT EVERYONE called her "Liz," which was a bit classier than "Lizzie," and what she preferred. "Lizzie" was old-fashioned, a name for middle-aged mothers and grandmothers. She wasn't so young, it was true, but being called "Liz" gave her a sense of identity, a person definitely not a "Lizzie."

She slid down the seat, crossed her arms, put her chin on her chest and decided to pout. This fifteen-passenger van filled with market girls could be an endurance test, the way these fifteen and sixteen year olds carried on. She knew it was all on account of Matthew Zook in the front seat, the tall handsome young man who owned and operated the "Dutch Eatery" at the huge Amish market in Lancaster, Pennsylvania.

Liz had worked as a cook, cashier, and waitress for eight years, doing a little (or a lot) of everything to keep the place running smoothly. She worked twelve-hour days tirelessly, faithfully. She loved her job, no matter who owned the restaurant, and found herself able to get along well with the two previous owners. But Matthew was another story.

Matthew was all of twenty-four years old, too young and too self-confident to be embarking on a venture in which he was clueless. He knew next to nothing about the place, had likely paid a fortune for the lease, was driven, intense, and extremely hard to get along with. Not to mention the fact that this gaggle of air-headed young girls that he attracted made her want to jump out the window.

He was ridiculously handsome, immensely self-centered, and grated on her nerves with his *grosfeelich* (proud) ways. But she was determined to remain loyal to the business, knowing if she left, the future of the Dutch Eatery was in serious jeopardy.

The Queen Street Market was an immense brick building, a former warehouse renovated to accommodate vendors selling everything from soft pretzels to leather goods. There was a beautiful produce stand, complete with timber framework, colorful displays of red, green, and yellow apples, pears, bananas, leafy greens, broccoli, and cauliflower. The produce stand was the center of the market, surrounded by smaller stands selling meats, cheeses, and sweet treats. There was a deli, a sub shop, and a few stands for handmade quilts and baby clothes.

Someone, usually a well-to-do non-Amish, or "English" as the Amish referred to outsiders, purchased the building for markets like this one, put the money into most of the remodeling, then leased each separate stand to vendors, many of them Amish. It was a good way to earn money and not forbidden by the church, as long as everyone respected the *ordnung* (rules), dressing and acting accordingly. There was always a bakery, the skills of Amish housewives put to good use, the loaves of bread and rolls, pies, cakes, and dozens of cookies and doughnuts turning into a tremendous volume of sold items. The markets buzzed with energy, the Amish folks enjoying the satisfaction of honest work, and the visitors appreciating the selection of unique goods.

At the Queen Street Market, scents of fresh pastries mixed with the aromas of roasting smoked ham, rotisserie chickens, and of course, the jumble of mouthwatering dishes from the Dutch Eatery. Liz loved all of it, hopping off the van between five and six in the morning, eager to turn on the grill and the oven, get the coffeemakers going. She loved the repetition of everyone knowing their place, everyone pulling together as a team. The day would go seamlessly if everyone did their share, and normally Liz would be the one to prod here, remind there, careful to be aware of damaged egos.

But Matthew was changing everything. He rearranged the kitchen, rewrote the menu, bought tablecloths for all the tables, and ordered peeled potatoes for home fries, which consequently turned out mushy, a fact that Liz's usual customers did not appreciate. She told him repeatedly that he should switch back to regular potatoes, but last week when she brought it up again, she saw the flash of anger in his eyes, the set of his jaw.

Today, she was determined to do better. Today, she would go his way, respect his authority, even if she had to fry the mushy potatoes till they were mashed potato patties. If he lost customers, well, it wasn't her worry. She was only an employee.

Three of the nine girls in the van worked for Matthew and every one of them was there because of him. They seemed to have no interest in hard work, but took every opportunity to get his undivided attention, which was maddening.

Today though, she would start off the day focused on God. She had prayed in faith, told Him she needed his help to get through the day, to stay by her side and let only soft, mellow words out of her mouth. Helpful, encouraging words, no matter the circumstances.

She went straight to the restroom, checked her appearance to be sure her hair and covering were in order before starting the day. She grimaced at the puffiness around her eyes, the dullness in the blue eyes that used to sparkle like diamonds. Her hair was brown streaked with blond, or blond streaked with brown, whichever one she preferred to think about. She had full lips, a wide mouth that once was given to quick smiles.

Matthew had made her life more difficult in recent months, but he wasn't the one responsible for stealing her joy, her youthful exuberance.

Only a couple of years ago her wedding had been planned, her blue dress sewn, pressed and hung in the closet, awaiting the day she and her beloved had planned together. November 7. A Thursday. But on September 13, he had begun to act strangely, agitated. By the time the evening was over, there were no wedding plans, nothing, only a hollow place where her heart used to be, the death knell of her love a lonesome gong that rang through her mind for the better part of a year.

And here she was, partially healed, mostly okay with the past, her faith strengthened and deepened by the polishing her spiritual life had received, her vessel shining like gold after having been put through the fire.

But it still hurt that, after breaking off their engagement, he then married her best friend at the time. It had taken him exactly eight weeks to ask Naomi for a date. She had said yes eagerly and gone on to enjoy a whirlwind romance, setting a date for their wedding while Liz still reeled from the sudden rejection.

Matthew searched her face as she entered the kitchen. She ignored him, pushed past to turn on the heat below the grill. Her green dress hung neatly to a few inches above the floor, her white apron accentuating her slim figure.

"Liz."

"Hmm?"

"Let's keep an eye on the potatoes today. I heard a customer say they were overcooked yesterday."

Irritation surged through her entire body, turning her cheeks pink. How many times had she told him the customers were unhappy about the stupid potatoes? And now he was informing her as if it was the first he'd heard of it, and worse, implying it was her fault. Without glancing in his direction, she told him as long as he bought peeled potatoes, he'd have mush.

"But I want to take this place to the next level," he said, leaning against the stainless steel table, crossing his arms—those tanned, muscled arms the other girls whispered about.

She couldn't contain her annoyance.

"Next level? You'll do well to rake in half the profit Bennie did."

Silence hovered uncomfortably.

"You don't like me, do you?" His voice was calm, which only made her feel more upset.

She kept her back turned, lifting a package of loose sausage from the commercial refrigerator.

"It doesn't matter if I like you or not. You're the boss." She reached to the top shelf for a heavy stainless steel kettle, set it on the stove, and turned. She met his eyes, a mixture of gray and green, surrounded by heavy eyelashes.

"You really think I should go back to unpeeled potatoes, don't you." It was a statement more than a question.

"Yes."

He shook his head, leaned forward and uncrossed his arms. "I just never thought they were that great."

"It's not about you. It's what the customers like and what they expect. Market people don't like change. If a stand changes hands, the business goes downhill."

He eyed her levelly.

"Ouch," he said softly.

"Whatever." She shrugged her shoulders, dumped a hefty amount of fresh sausage in the heating kettle.

"That's an awful lot of sausage. I have to make a profit, you know."

"Look. You want to lose customers, start skimping on the sausage in the gravy, okay?"

"But sausage isn't cheap."

"If you want to cut costs, get rid of the tablecloths and stop paying to get them washed and pressed every day. People don't come here for fancy tablecloths. They come for good food and good service. Where is Priscilla with the cart from the walk-in cooler?"

"I'll get her."

Liz snorted in an unladylike manner, realizing how quickly her commitment to a better attitude had gone out the window. When Ruthie stuck her head through the door, Liz snapped at her about not filling the salt and pepper shakers. Matthew irritated her and her irritation was seeping into her directions to Ruthie, even after she'd been so sure her day would be infused by God's love and compassion.

It was men in general. They all irritated her since the fateful day her love had called off the wedding and gone gallivanting off with her best friend. All men thought they had the God-given right to lord it over the weaker sex, the poor flabbergasted girls who made sheep's eyes at them in the hopes of securing their affection. She was aware of her warped attitude and didn't care. She had plenty of reason to dislike men. And Matthew was no exception.

She had no time to think about anything but work after that. She was focused on the breakfast preparation, sliding homemade biscuits into the oven, filling trays with bacon, barking orders to Eva, the timid new girl who was painfully slow. As the orders piled in, she was fully occupied, unaware of anything beyond the swinging doors.

She flipped eggs, pancakes, made omelets, crumbled biscuits and ladled gravy over them. Eva buttered toast and pancakes, slid orders out the window, and mostly kept her eyes on Matthew.

Liz found herself humming as she worked, her spirits lifting as she moved swiftly, feeling the rhythm of the busy breakfast shift. She laughed at Eva when she threw a sausage patty on the grill, felt herself drawn to the girl's dry humor. When breakfast was over, she cleaned up, reminded Eva to fill the Hobart to capacity, to scrape the worst of the baked-on food from the kettles and pans.

"How's it going?"

This from Matthew, entering the kitchen with a swagger she knew to mean only one thing: there had been a good crowd for breakfast and he was pleased with his success.

"Alright."

She was scraping the grill top with a metal sponge clasped in tongs, the vicious cleaner a threat to anyone's health, she guaranteed.

"Why don't you leave that 'til lunch is over?"

"I told you."

"Look. That grill cleaner isn't cheap. Leave it. Scrape it down. You can make burgers on a dark grill.

Liz worked the residue with a scraper, upended the vinegar jug without answering.

"Did you hear me?"

"I heard you."

"Do it then. Tomorrow. No grill cleaning 'til the end of the day."

Liz gritted her teeth, said nothing. Out of the corner of her eye, she saw him flash Eva a smile, one of those devastating smiles Eva would cherish far too deeply and far too long.

"Need any help in here?" he asked in a voice as oily as unwashed hair.

"I don't care," Eva giggled.

"What are you doing?" he asked.

"Chopping green peppers."

"Careful there, you'll chop your pretty fingers."

Liz wiped the stainless steel tabletop furiously. She felt the heat in her face, thought she actually might go up in flames. His ego was absolutely out of control. She pushed past him to get to the mop sink for a plastic bucket, without looking at him.

"Let me get that," he offered.

She felt his presence, too close, too confident.

"I know what I'm doing. Just . . ." She made a shooing motion, a sort of scooping with her right arm.

* * *

By the end of the day, the numbing exhaustion had crept through her arms and legs. Clearly, there had been an increase in customers, which had served the purpose of increasing Matthew's confidence substantially and undermining her own proclamation that he was running things poorly. Soup pots were drained, the hoagie maker was littered with sandwich-making residue, and globs of mayonnaise and mustard dotted the countertops.

She had done without her normal fifteen-minute breaks. During cleanup, she told him in clipped tones he needed to hire another girl. With Thanksgiving and Christmas coming on, the cold would bring more hungry shoppers, the people out and about over the holiday season.

"I can't afford to pay more help."

"You can't afford not to."

"Why is that?"

"We can't keep up the quality of the service Bennie had with only four of us."

"Bennie, Bennie, Bennie. That's all I hear. You must think the guy was really something."

"He had a very successful business."

"Then why did he quit?"

"His family. His wife is not in the best of health. She didn't like market at all, stayed home with the five children, and it was too much for her."

"That's why I never married."

Liz had to be very careful, putting another slice of toast on top of the bacon, tomato, and lettuce, before taking up the serrated knife to cut it diagonally. She sat down at a table, grimaced as she saw the stains on the tablecloth, frowned at the empty napkin dispenser, the smudges on the glass salt and pepper shakers.

"Look at this. Would you want to sit down at one of these tables?"

He sat down across from her, too close and much too confident. His hands were tanned, well formed, the nails clipped and clean.

"What's wrong with it?"

"Look at the dirty tablecloth, the napkin holder, everything. Where were the girls?"

"Which one? Eva helps you. Ruthie and Priscilla are kept busy."

Liz took a large bite out of her sandwich, chewed with a hand over her mouth, tapping lightly. She caught him watching her, couldn't help responding when his eyes crinkled with amusement. How could one man contain every masculine asset? No wonder he irritated her with his supreme sense of self. Seriously, the man was so handsome. She swallowed, took another large bite, didn't bother covering her mouth at all. She was too hungry, had had no time to eat all day, and that really was illegal.

She told him as she popped the top off a can of Coke and poured it over ice, drank thirstily, and burped quietly into a napkin before starting in on the second half of her sandwich.

"I'm not hiring another girl."

"Then I quit."

"You can't do that, Liz."

"I can, and I will. You can't run out of homemade soups and sliced meat before the dinner rush. You can't have a menu if you can't deliver the food. It's that simple."

He sighed. "You do nothing for a man's confidence."

"Oh, you have plenty of that."

He did hire another person, an overweight aging Amish woman from below Quarryville who flopped into the van one morning, crossed her hands across her rounded stomach, and fell asleep the minute they hit the interstate highway.

Her name was Annie, and she turned out to be the most refreshing person Liz had ever met. She wore her white market apron like a clean, billowing sail, wore colorful dresses with puffy sleeves and snaps down the front. Her black Crocs made little squeaks as she moved swiftly from the freezer to fridge to stove and back again. She talked constantly in a loud tone, but she never dwelt on herself, only on others. A great band of interesting people made up her world, and she loved freely, unabashedly. She talked about her husband, her neighbor down the street, her miniature poodle, her married girls and their husbands, her grandchildren, especially her special one, a girl with Down syndrome named Margaret.

"Margaret, Liz. Now really. They call her Margie. As in margarine. I call her Blue Bonnet. Get it, Liz? As in Blue Bonnet margarine."

She fastened her twinkling brown eyes on Liz's face, waiting for her response, and Liz was awash in genuine laughter. That's what Annie was. Refreshing.

Liz's job became more manageable, her life easier as the green leaves of summer took on the jaded look of advancing autumn. Pumpkins ripened in the field, busy housewives gathered every tomato, bean, head of cabbage, and late corn and made great kettles of vegetable soup, ladled it into jars, and cold packed it in double burner canners steaming away atop propane-fired, outdoor gas stoves.

At home on the farm close to Strasburg, Liz stayed occupied with the last of the fall canning, and the painting that meant someone was preparing for a wedding. It was, in fact, her younger sister Marianne whose special day was the Tuesday before Thanksgiving. She was marrying her best friend, a young man she had started dating at sixteen and never looked back. She was one of the fortunate ones, the girls blessed with the deep, abiding love that would last a lifetime, her husband always being the center of her life.

Liz talked about this phenomenon to Annie, who of course, got quick tears of compassion. Her nose reddened, and her mouth turned wobbly as she told Liz that she remembered well when Ab sie Becky told her about Ray breaking up with Liz only two short months before the wedding.

Liz picked up a plastic spoon, grimaced as she tasted the chicken corn soup, then turned the burner low.

"It must have been horrible." Annie spoke as if she really felt the pain of the heartbreak.

"It was. I don't like men to this day. I don't trust any of them. I'll never date again, and I will never get married."

Annie bent to retrieve stalks of celery, her great backside a wall of purple, almost as wide as the refrigerator itself.

She grasped the bundle of stalks firmly as she held it below the faucet, shook her head as she thumped it down on a cutting board.

"You can't say that. Bitterness will eat away your soul the way cancer does to a body. You don't know what God has for you."

God did have a fine young man for her, or so she'd thought. And He had tricked her into believing that for two and a half years. She had a right to feel a little resentful. Still, she knew her faith had been deepened, the way she no longer felt the need to understand everything, but rather, a sense of giving herself to a Higher Knowledge. God knew her heart, He knew every fiber of her being, so if that was the case, what did she have to fear? It was perfectly okay to remain single, even if she lived in a culture where being married and having children was what most girls aspired to from the time they were toddlers.

The shock, the hurt, the impending depression, the days it took superhuman effort to put her feet on the floor of her bedroom, to lift her heavy body from the mattress, walk to the bathroom across the hallway, lift the white curtain and gaze down on a colorless world. . . . No, she would never forget. Taking another risk was not worth the pain. The remembered humiliation of watching him stand beside Naomi on their wedding day, knowing many eyes were upon her at that moment, curious eyes, wondering how she could look so stoic. *Poor girl. Poor*

Liz. But they couldn't imagine the reality of what she'd been through, was going through still.

So, yes, it was behind her now and it would be foolish to get swept up in another romance. She honestly didn't know if she could survive the pain and humiliation a second time.

She had her family. Her parents were very dear to her heart, as were her sisters and her cousins. She was surrounded by friends and loved ones. What more could she ask for?

"Did I tell you about my daughter's tumble down the cellar steps?" Annie asked, as she chopped carrots for fresh vegetable soup.

"No."

Liz was preoccupied, squinting at the three remaining orders. Perhaps if she was lucky, she could have a fifteen-minute break after this.

"Sylvia is like me. A bit round and really *schoos-lich* (hasty). She was carrying a tray of freshly canned applesauce, tripped on the second step, and fell headlong. She broke her shoulder. They live in Nittany, you know. And Aaron—that's her husband—he's not real *gootmānich* (kind). He was just disgusted.

Oh I pitied her so *veesht* (badly). He doesn't like her to be so fat. Well, I shouldn't say 'fat.' She's just round, like I am. Not really fat. I think 'fat' is such a crass word. Anyway, they had a *hesslich* (serious) hospital bill, and he had to do the washing. Can't imagine a husband doing the washing. Especially not him. I don't want to talk about my son-in-law, but he's sort of dumb. She even fixes her own washing machine. The wringer, you know, when it pops. He just can't figure things out. She suffered *hesslich* with that shoulder, and her baby Evan only nine months old. Can you imagine naming a boy Evan? But whatever. He cried and cried when she couldn't pick him up. Poor, poor baby. Oh, I pitied him."

The swinging doors were pushed in, and Matthew appeared, his face very serious.

"Liz, can I talk to you for a moment?"

Chapter Two

"CAN YOU COME WITH ME, PLEASE?"

Shocked into obedience, Liz complied. She found herself in an office of sorts and sat down when he motioned to a chair then sat behind an old, battered desk.

"Have you noticed anything strange about Priscilla?"

Liz wrinkled her brow, thinking about the past few weeks. Priscilla was the head waitress, the first to be hired of the three teenaged employees and the oldest among them. She was one of the harder workers with a good head on her shoulders, smart, quick to observe the needs of her customers. But being in the kitchen never left much time to keep track of the waitresses. Priscilla was quiet, not a beauty by any standard, but had an open, innocent look about her, her wavy blond hair her biggest asset.

Liz met his eyes, noticed the concern.

"Not really. Why?"

"This is serious business, but I don't know who else I can confide in. I think she is meeting a married man."

Liz felt the color drain from her face. Her eyes opened wide as her mouth fell open.

"No. She wouldn't do such a thing. Who? Is he Amish?"

"No, he's English. I'm so afraid for her. I don't think she knows what she's getting into. In fact, I doubt if she knows he's married, but I've seen him in here with his wife."

"Are you sure it was his wife?"

"He introduced us. Look, I know the guy. I would never have thought in a million years. It's real, I'm afraid."

"How do you know?"

For the first time ever, Matthew looked embarrassed. He avoided her eyes, fidgeted in his chair. "It's . . . it's embarrassing. I'm ashamed to tell you."

"Then don't."

"What should I do?"

"That depends."

"What do you mean by that?"

"If you're positive something is going on, then by all means approach her, call her out. She needs to know this is wrong. But if you're only guessing, then you need to watch her for a while, see if it continues."

"What about contacting her parents?"

"I don't know her parents. I have no idea what her home life is like. I'd feel bad if this all went the wrong way. Look, I have to get back. Annie can't do everything on her own."

"Help me watch her for a while. Please."

For once, he seemed humbled, a bit unsure of his position. She gave him the assurance of her smile, a nod, letting her eyes speak the words he needed to hear.

"Hey, thanks. Appreciate it."

* * *

As she carried a tray from the kitchen to a side table for her lunch break, she allowed herself a sweeping view of the dining area. A few patrons were enjoying a late lunch, the people in the central area of the market walking along, some of them in a rush as they excused themselves past browsers who paid them no attention. She saw nothing unusual, until she noticed Priscilla's absence.

Stay calm, observe, she told herself.

She opened a package of saltines, then another, before dipping her spoon into the creamy seafood chowder. Halfway through her bowl, she noticed a red-cheeked, disheveled Priscilla hurry along the aisle on her way to the restroom. Her heart sank, then began racing haphazardly. Did Matthew actually know what he was stalking about? She sincerely hoped she was not becoming embroiled in a situation beyond her control. It would be so terribly hard to see this girl come to harm.

She scraped the last of her soup before getting up and putting her napkin in the trash. She turned to go to the kitchen when she caught a flash of blue and white. Priscilla was moving quickly, back to the register, where she had asked Ruthie to take over for her.

"Thanks," she said, too loudly.

"Any time," Ruthie answered kindly.

Priscilla looked up in time to see Liz watching her. She flashed a self-conscious smile of acknowledgment before bending behind the register. Liz stayed where she was, waiting till she raised her head, then gave her a level stare the minute she looked at her again.

The remainder of the day passed with burrs of unease pricking her thoughts, and in the van, she was terribly aware of Priscilla's chatter. But nothing she said provided evidence for or against Matthew's claims.

* * *

On Sunday morning, dressed in the traditional church attire, she noticed the brilliant autumnal colors, the deep blue of the sky, the clouds like cotton balls dappled across it. The air held the faint scent of dying grass and falling leaves, the crisp feeling of a frosty night.

She rode to church with her brother Samuel, a youth of fifteen, tall, lanky, and full of every good thing life contained. To him, the world was a solid white canvas on which he would splatter whatever colorful event came up next.

"Hey, you know what, Liz? I am one good ball player. Did you know they're thinking of making me team captain? Like, I get to call the shots? Boy, that should impress Priscilla. She is so cute, and I think she likes me. She acts like it. All the girls like me. Almost. Hey, you know what? She is the best at volleyball. She can jump higher than any girl I know. If she was English, I bet you she'd be a cheerleader. Oh . . .look at Ernie's half-dead horse. Poor guy. He needs another horse, but their dad is mean. I mean *mean*. Ernie is Priscilla's brother."

Liz's voice was sharper than she intended. "Where does this Priscilla live?"

"I dunno. Somewhere here around Lancaster, same as everyone else."

Priscilla was an uncommon name, unlike Martha or Sarah or Rebecca. Could this girl be the same one she worked with? *Oh my*, she thought, with a sort of tired resignation. *The plot thickens.*

"Why is Ernie's father mean?" she ventured slowly.

"He just is. He got whooped when he was fifteen. You know what for? For letting the water spigot open in the forebay. He didn't do it on purpose. His pap whooped him so hard he couldn't sit right for a while."

"You think it's true?"

"Sure it's true. Why would he lie? Ernie doesn't say *schnitzas* (lies)."

The first sermon was based on family life, basically, the minister a young man in his thirties. He spoke of the need to show kindness and patience, to discipline with love, and to allow the children access to Jesus, the way the Bible taught them all. Liz found the message deeply stirring, especially the part where he explained the insecurity children often displayed, living with a lack of kindness and understanding. She found herself wondering about Priscilla. Was Matthew being paranoid? Jealous? But he'd said it was embarrassing, and certainly looked uncomfortable telling her about it.

As thoughts tend to do in a three-hour church service, she found them wandering again and again, processing the information her garrulous brother offered at random. She certainly had not asked to be drawn into this situation, and she didn't want to meddle, but she felt responsible now that Matthew had confided in her.

She found herself forsaking God to guide Priscilla as the congregation knelt for the silent first prayer. She hardly knew the girl, but something tugged at her heart, so she prayed.

The second sermon was conducted by the home bishop, the one responsible to look over his flock of thirty-one families who lived in close proximity. All over Lancaster County there were small areas called districts, each containing a group of twenty to thirty or so families. When a district grew to forty or more, the church was divided, meaning the ministry decided on a landmark, a road, a creek, a route that put a dividing line between the large group. After that, there would be the solemn task of ordaining more ministers, another deacon, one who would be chosen by the drawing of lots, the way they had done so many years ago in the Bible. In this way, the Amish churches grew and flourished far beyond anyone's expectations, the boundaries reaching to Maryland and extending in every direction.

The elderly bishop spoke of caring for another in love, explaining the question, "Am I my brother's keeper?" Yes, yes, in love we care for one another, in times of grief, in times of sickness and the onslaught of trials. He explained in detail how the love of Christ is revealed through acts of kindness. *Barmherzichkeit* (compassion).

Priscilla wandered in and out of Liz's thoughts. She felt an uncommon emotion, tears threatened.

Lord, I'd rather not get involved, she pleaded. But she knew she already was.

She helped set the tables after services, spread tablecloths down the length of benches turned into tables by setting them on trestles designed for this purpose. She carried trays of peanut butter spread, jelly, spreadable cheese, butter. There were platters of bread, dried apple pie, and fresh sweet bologna and smoked ham, red beets, and thinly sliced pickles. All of it was traditional, the same foods that had been served after services for hundreds of years. She had eaten bits of peanut butter *brot* (bread) on her mother's lap as a toddler, had enjoyed the same Sunday lunch as an older child, waiting hungrily till the men had all eaten at one table, the women at another, and then the cups, saucers, and utensils were washed and set back on the table for the teenagers and children above the age of nine.

Liz served coffee, filled water glasses, then made sure the pies and bread were replenished as needed. A group of women stood at tables with tubs of hot soapy water, clean rinse water, and tea towels for drying—the dish-washing station. A lively chatter surrounded everything, women fussing like biddy hens, men standing along the wall, their conversation adding to the drone of fellowship.

She spoke to her friend Esther as they were seated at the second table, smiled at the row of young girls filing onto the long benches. This was home, her life, her church, a place she loved and belonged, a secure group of intertwined lives and loves. Esther had become her dearest friend, one of the few people in the world she felt she could confide in. She was fun while still being down-to-earth, and she was easy to be around.

After the meal, Liz set out to find her brother, who she was sure was hanging out with a group of boys somewhere nearby. He was always the center of attention, always impressing the others with embellished stories and wild antics. She found him beside the silo, his arms whirring like a windmill, no doubt elaborating on some questionable venture or other.

He looked up. "What?"

"You ready?"

"Yeah. You know where I'm parked?"

She nodded. "Esther's coming along."

"Okay." He nodded agreeably. Liz knew he enjoyed sitting close to all her girlfriends. A buggy is not very spacious, which was fine with him. Of course, the ride home was flecked with his exploits, real or imagined, his language peppered with English phrases he considered very cool. Liz cringed, but Esther seemed to enjoy him immensely, her laugh ringing out repeatedly.

As they showered and dressed for the youth gathering, the sun slid behind a bank of gray clouds, sending an overcast sheen across the bedroom. Liz snapped on her battery lamp before parting the sheer curtains and snapping up the blind.

"Oh boy. If it rains, it'll be a boring afternoon and evening."

Esther snorted, a sound that always made Liz burst out laughing. "Every gathering is boring for you. Rain, shine, or whatever."

Liz drew the fine-toothed comb through her hair, turned her head to the left to view the result, then picked up a can of hairspray before applying a liberal amount. "I'm old. A bit jaded, I suppose. Every Sunday is the same old thing. I declare, if I ever see another pan of meat loaf with that sweet ketchup slop smeared over the top, I'll throw up."

"I, for one, love meatloaf. With mashed potatoes and brown gravy. You're just grouchy."

Liz put a clip barrette behind her ear, then began on the opposite side. "Seriously, Esther, I'm not. It's just the fact that we do the same thing over and over, and you know as well as I do, there is no one in our youth gathering containing the slightest possibility of marriage for me. They're all so young."

"You need a better job. One that challenges your mind. Like teaching. Market is all you've ever done."

"I love market. Always have."

"True. You have. But it's such a mindless thing."

"Mindless? Try tending the grill with dozens of orders piling up and no end in sight. That is not mindless."

"But you're always with the same people."

"No more than teachers are. The wait staff changes all the time, actually."

Esther grinned, gathering her belongings and zipped them into her duffle bag. "How many hours are you planning on spending on your hair?"

"You never know. Prince Charming might show up unexpectedly, and I may be swept off my feet at the ripe old age of twenty-two years . . . plus a few months, and I don't know how many days."

Esther gave her a mock shiver. "Stop that! It's so morbid. You talk like you're at your own funeral."

"That's not funny."

But they both laughed.

"Well," said Esther from the mirror, where she was giving herself one last adjustment. "I have full intentions of having the time of my life. The best is yet to come, Liz. Think positive. If nothing seems to be going well, it's because we don't get the whole picture. God sees our whole future. You know that. Right?"

"Right, Esther. I actually believe being a single girl for the rest of my life is His plan, so that's what I'll be. I'll always have market."

"You love your job that much, really?"

"I do."

* * *

The long gravel driveway contained gray and black carriages lined up on both sides, the space by the barn filled with them, horses being unhitched or led to the barn, groups of colorful girls like bright blossoms dotting the gray and black, with the white metal-clad barn in the background. Behind the red brick house, a lively game of volleyball was already underway, colorful shirts and dresses accented with black trousers and belt aprons.

It was called "the supper," a traditional Dutch word for the youth gathering at the home of a member of the *rumschpringa*. The meal would be served at approximately six o'clock. Long tables were laden

with tremendous amounts of food, usually everything served from huge stainless steel kettles and
roasters, salads in the biggest available bowls. There
were often more than a hundred young people, plus
the married couples who came to help with the cooking, and to oversee the behavior, especially if one of
their own was among the *rumschpringa*.

After long lines of youth had filled their paper
plates and finished their dessert, it was back to volleyball or other games, before it was time to begin the
Sunday evening hymn singing. *Die singin'*, the time
of singing German hymns, the young men lined up
along one side of the table, the girls on the other,
their voices blending in harmony as they sang praises
from *die lieda bücha* (songbooks). Parents sat along
both sides in the back, their voices blending with the
youthful chorus, children dashing about or sitting
quietly on laps, their eyelids drooping as sleepiness
began to take over.

Liz and Esther were no newcomers, but one of
die eltry maide (the older girls). They talked with the
married women, offered to help prepare supper, then
gradually drifted out to watch the volleyball players.

Liz wondered vaguely whether she had ever been quite as silly as some of these young girls. They were so flirtatious, just plain ridiculous. She felt sour, even self-righteous, as if she was so much better at the ripe old age of twenty-two. She berated her wayward thoughts and pressed her lips into a straight line to take control of them.

She was aware of someone behind her. She caught a whiff of men's cologne before she heard a familiar voice say, "Doesn't look as if we have much of a chance."

Matthew? Matthew Zook?

She froze. Seated on the grass, her legs tucked beneath her, she wished she could turn invisible. She had never spoke to him, even seen him, outside of market or the market van. Hopefully he would not recognize her, turn away if there was no opening to play volleyball. Her heart thudded loudly in her chest.

"Is that you, Liz?" he asked, his voice unmistakeable.

She turned to look up at him, felt the slow flush spread across her cheeks. For a moment, she imagined she would choke if she tried to speak, but after swallowing, clearing her throat, she said, "It's me," in a weak, gravelly voice.

To her consternation, he squatted down beside her, his hands dangling from his bent knees.

"How's it going, Liz?"

How was it going? Her heart was racing the way she imagined hearts did prior to cardiac arrest. Her eyes were blurred with a strange inability to focus properly and her face was flushed with what she feared was an obscene color of purple. One thought raced frantically through her mind, why was he here? Was he seeing one of the young women?

"Okay," she managed, giving him a quick glance.

Oh my. He was so ridiculously good-looking, dressed in his Sunday best.

He pointed his chin toward Esther.

"Will you introduce me to your friend?"

"Oh. Uh . . . sorry. This is Esther. Esther, Matthew."

"Hi."

"Hello. Good to meet you." Matthew got to his feet. "And this is Henry King."

"Hello," from Esther, who had the good sense to rise gracefully to her feet, put out a hand to shake the newcomer's extended one.

Liz got to her feet with what she hoped was a graceful move, but she actually felt like a cow, all clumsiness and scattered limbs. She did not extend a hand but met his eyes briefly with a small, "Hello."

"Henry and I go way back, like sixth grade. We've been friends for years. How about you two?"

Esther looked at Liz, who smiled back at her. It was easier to talk as long as she kept her eyes on her friend.

"We've been friends for only a year or so. Is it a year and a half?"

In her blunt manner, Esther wrinkled her brow. "I don't know. How long has it been since Ray broke up with you?"

Liz could only hope for a miracle, such as the ground opening up and swallowing her completely. She felt the same miserable flush creeping into her cheeks, kept her eyes lowered to a safe spot, which seemed to be the tips of her shoes. The silence stretched as taut as a bowstring.

"Um . . . I don't know. Almost a year and a half," she mumbled finally.

"Yeah, probably. Liz had her wedding all planned. Sewing done. Everything. Ray broke up with her a month or so before the wedding and went on to marry her best friend. No one should have to go through that. But after that, we started hanging out more, and now we're best friends!"

Matthew was clearly taken by surprise. "Wow. He must not have been too bright. Who would do something like that to a girl like you?"

Liz was speechless, the phrase slowly filtering into her understanding. Did he mean it the way it sounded?

Henry repeated, "Wow."

"Oh yeah, it was a genuine bummer. Like the apocalypse for Liz. But she had more bravery than anyone I know. Courage. Just climbed right out of her loss like you wouldn't believe."

"Let's change the subject, okay?" Liz suggested.

"So we're all a bit long in the tooth, huh?" Henry asked, grinning broadly. Turning to Esther, he asked how old she was and whether she was dating, which shocked Esther. It was a bold question considering they'd just met.

"I'm hovering dangerously close to becoming a singleton," she told him with her flash of good humor.

He laughed. Matthew smiled, his smile deepening and widening to a genuine grin of appreciation.

"So you're thirty-nine and holding?" he asked

"Yep, I am."

Henry said quickly, "You know, this is so boring. These suppers. Why don't we all go for a walk? Maybe to the park?"

"Good idea," Matthew said.

Esther looked at Liz, raised one eyebrow comically, rolled her eyes, and clasped her hands. Liz nodded.

"Okay, lead the way."

Many eyes watched the foursome walk out the carriage-lined drive, but soon lost sight as they disappeared behind a line of trees. The volleyball games continued, the crowd of youth preoccupied with each other.

Liz and Esther walked ahead of the two young men, each silently hoping the coverings on their heads were straight, their aprons centered precisely with small steel pins intact, no runs in their stockings. Here was an unexpected turn of events. Henry was quite a presentable young man. He was a bit short, but his straight dark hair accentuating his wide, dark eyes, his ready smile and open, friendly face. No one could match Matthew's perfection entirely, but Henry came close.

They settled around a rustic picnic table, the late afternoon sun turning the brilliant trees into a kaleidoscope of orange, yellow, and red, the grass taking on a golden sheen, the green electrified by the slanting rays of golden light. Conversation flowed easily, with Esther doing most of the talking. Henry was the quietest of all of them, but when he did speak, he was direct and very pleasant. Perhaps not as confident as Matthew, but still friendly.

"What is hard for me to understand," Henry said finally, "is where you two were till now?"

Matthew grinned, told him to take it easy, he'd scare them away, which did nothing to deter his enthusiasm. "I work with Liz," he said still smiling.

"You mean, I work for you."

"Sometimes I'm not sure who works for whom, as much as you boss me around," he said, his eyes shining playfully and lingering on Liz's face.

Chapter Three

MONDAY MORNING BROUGHT BRILLIANT sunshine, frosty breezes, and the kitchen drenched in yellow light. Liz lingered with her mother over steaming cups of coffee, the breakfast dishes scattered across the countertop, the tablecloth littered with shoofly crumbs, bits of egg, and crusts of toast.

The three school-aged children were shrugging into their coats, arguing over the necessity of wearing them at all. Jason smashed his straw hat on his head, scowled at Suzanna, and said it was chillier than it looked out there, that even the ducks were cold, staying completely out of the pond that morning.

"How do you know?" Suzanna mumbled, her chin buried in her sweater as she struggled with her buttons.

"They were all in the forebay."

Sarah flashed her brother a look of exasperation. "That's what I stepped in when I fed the pony. You need to get rid of those ducks."

"I love my ducks. It's not their fault you were clumsy."

"Bye, Mam. Bye, Liz!" Suzanna called.

"Goodbye, children. Be careful," Mam answered, as she swiveled her chair to watch the troop of three head out the door.

"Bye! Bye!" they called back, before breaking into a run.

"Their endless energy," Mam sighed.

"And endless talking," Liz answered, laughing.

Mam shook her head, but there was a proud light in her eyes. She took off her glasses, replaced them after rubbing one eye. Her face was unlined, still amazingly youthful after eight children and the care of a big farmhouse and large lawn and garden, a herd of dairy cows, and all that went with the work of a successful farm. Her white covering was neat and clean, her hair rolled back along the sides, her green everyday dress showing years of wear.

Two of her teenaged daughters were sleeping in on a Monday morning. Marianne and Sylvia had spent Saturday night with friends, getting only a few hours of sleep. Jobs would await them when they appeared, but Mam allowed them the extra hours of rest. Samuel was already hitching up the four-horse hitch, preparing to bale corn fodder most of the day.

"So what will it be?" Mam asked. "Housecleaning or finishing up the garden?"

"Why don't we do the garden today?" Liz asked. "We won't have these nice days much longer."

"Church is here in two weeks, Liz. I'm a bit panicked about the housecleaning."

"Really, Mam? The whole house doesn't have to be done. Who's going to know the difference?"

Her mother gasped. It was unthinkable, leaving a house half-cleaned before church.

Housecleaning meant walls and curtains washed, window blinds taken down and wiped with soapy water, windows washed inside and out, even upstairs where you turned yourself into a pretzel reaching up or down on the outside of the window. Bedding was swirled in the wringer washer, hung out to dry, along with rugs, doilies, and anything washable in every room. Drawers were emptied and wiped out, articles replaced before the dresser itself was wiped down with furniture polish and a soft rag. The entire house was finished in this fashion, bathrooms scoured and scrubbed, ceilings and walls without a fleck of fly dirt or grease smudges. The kitchen stove and refrigerator were pulled away from the wall, spider webs and dust bunnies attacked with a brush and dustpan before being followed up with a hot soapy rag.

Housecleaning meant a beef roast in the oven, with potatoes and carrots, or a pot of tomato soup and grilled cheese sandwiches. The washline was filled and refilled, white sheets and colorful quilts like hula dancers in the fickle breeze.

This was every spring and every fall, with the announcement of church services to be held at their place like a whip goading Mam on. The thought of a stray spider web or a smudged window being spied by someone like Aaron sie Rachel was simply too humiliating, so it was onward ho! There was a reputation to uphold, and laziness was next to gluttony as far as every *fliesich* (industrious) housewife was concerned.

Then there was the matter of three teenaged girls unsatisfied with Mam's old-fashioned, outdated shower curtain and decorations, expressing the necessity of making a trip to Target.

"Why Target? It's too expensive. Wal-Mart is just fine."

The girls rolled their eyes, knowing that if they let their mam do the shopping the shower curtain would be the cheapest brand available and the wrong color and wrong style.

They took it upon themselves to paint both bathrooms, buy the new rugs and shower curtains, add the wall décor they preferred. Mam shrugged her shoulders, said she liked it, but didn't care one way or another. A bathroom was just a bathroom, to her, and didn't the bishop discourage decorating?

Mam was like that. A bit tight-lipped if the girls stepped out of her boundary lines, which were too stringent, according to Marianne and Sylvia, who got away with much more than Liz ever did, of which they were reminded frequently. They wore their dresses long, their sleeves tight and short, which was the style of the day, and Mam never batted an eye, saying it was modest, so what if it was the style? And Liz felt quite the martyr having been out of style completely when she turned sixteen years old and had to join the *rumschpringa* with a shorter dress and looser, longer sleeves than her contemporaries.

But it was life, and she loved her mother so much. She knew most families learned together as the children grew. Amish folks lived with more rules than non-Amish, but there would always be the styles that came and went, the liberals pushing the envelope of what was acceptable and what was not, the conservatives staying well within the boundaries and often *fa-denking* (criticizing) those who were more liberal. Human nature abounded, even within the safety of the *ordnung*, but with the love of Christ, the striving to live together in peace and harmony, most districts grew and flourished. Change came slowly, but as the decades came and went, the expectations did shift.

Mam remembered well the filling of kerosene lamps, the washing and polishing of glass chimneys, the bathroom lit by the dim yellow glow. Now there were the DeWalt battery lamps, bright and white, illuminating every sag and wrinkle, revealing grease stains and unironed coverings. In July and August heat, there were whirring, undulating fans in every corner of the kitchen, all run from these miraculous little rechargeable batteries. There were blenders and coffee makers, mixers and steam irons, even wringer washers run by these little wonders.

Large solar panels dotted rooftops, the energy directed to battery packs. Though some argued they were a source of electricity, they were also off-grid, so it was tolerated, accepted by some more than others.

But the fundamental beliefs stayed, the way church services, weddings, and funerals were directed, the horses and buggies clopping peacefully down country roads, the modest dress, apart from the world. And yet the world crept in, modernity nudging here and there, especially in attitudes and opinions, the sly wiles of the devil convincing indeed.

God provided minsters, young men filled with the Holy Spirit, led to exhort and encourage, to preach the gospel in all its unfettered glory, leaving the congregations filled with earnest desire to please God, to remain thankful for saving grace. And the churches grew.

Farms were sold, farmers losing their livelihood because they were simply unable to make a decent living. Their way of life was destroyed by low milk prices and exorbitant feed prices. In place of farms, there were more shops and stores, greenhouses, contractors and roofers, a new way of life for a great percentage of the plain people.

Luckily, if only by the grace of God, the home farm could still earn a decent living for Dat and Mam, the farm handed down to him from his prosperous father.

Liz straightened her back, looked along the bare soil, the garden cart filled with heavy tomato and pepper plants. This garden had been here for over a hundred years, the soil dark and loose, filled with nutrients, rich and loamy. The petunias still bloomed in a staggered row, but they would be removed today, it being only a matter of time till a killing frost turned them into a brown, slimy mush.

"Mam, if I ever have my own garden, I will never, ever plant bubblegum petunias. You can tell exactly which home is Amish by the row of pink petunias."

"Horse and buggy Mennonites," Mam said sourly, hurling a heavy pepper plant onto the garden cart.

"Well. Them, too."

"What do you have against them? They're easy to grow, colorful. They're pretty."

"They're everywhere."

"Well, if you ever have your own garden, you don't need to plant them."

"What do you mean '*if* you ever'?"

Mam laughed outright, a high cracking sound of delight. "Why? Is there a chance?"

Liz laughed too. "No, of course not.

But was there, really, no chance? Liz relived the late afternoon, the golden glow, the beauty around her, still etched in her mind. She felt ashamed of the way she felt, slowly admitting even to herself, the pull of attraction. She realized she was mesmerized by his hand movements, the ripple of honed muscle beneath the tanned skin on his forearms. The neat press of his trousers, the fit of his black vest. And was there ever better taste than a white, short-sleeved shirt setting off the color of his face and hair? His eyes looking straight into hers were just too much.

Had there really been any sign that he was attracted to her?

Yes. A resounding yes.

Both young men said they planned on joining the Cardinals, the group Esther and she belonged to. There were thousands of youth all over Lancaster County, so they were divided into separate groups, given names for identification, and supervised by concerned parents to stop the ever-intruding flow of low morals, of drugs and alcohol and every other wile of the devil.

Esther, being the outspoken person she was, upon hearing this intention, promptly asked, "Why would you do that?"

And Henry caught Matthew's eye and winked boldly. This was the incident Liz carried with her, replaying in her mind's eye.

The day was perfect, the tinge of frost in the air, the limp tomato plants a testimony to the damage already done.

The shelves in the cellar were lined with freshly folded newspaper and gleaming, colorful jars of vegetables and fruit displayed from floor to ceiling. There was the usual array of peaches, pears, apple-sauce, sour cherry pie filling. Plus the green beans, red beets, pickles, tomatoes, spaghetti sauce, salsa, relishes, and jams. It was a veritable store of riches. All the hard work of gardening and canning during the heat of summer left a deep sense of accomplishment in October.

* * *

The garden was cleaned and oats sowed for a cover crop, so they turned to housecleaning, starting in the attic. The perfect blue October sky had turned fickle, with scudding dark clouds, rain pelting on the roofs of the farm, water gushing from white spouting, ducks flapping happily as they spread their wings and quacked noisily.

It would be a perfect day to go through boxes in the attic, Mam announced, draining her coffee cup in that no-nonsense manner, which meant, "Get up and get going." Marianne and Sylvia weren't there, so it was just the two of them again.

The DeWalt lamps were hung from nails pounded into exposed rafters, and the rain made a dull shushing sound on the roof. It was cold but comfortable wearing a sweater with sleeves rolled to her elbows.

There were a few stinkbugs, some dead flies, and a few spider webs, but mostly the attic appeared clean, the boxes and totes stacked neatly. But, no, Mam thought the little girls had been up here more often than anyone knew, so they better check some of these boxes.

The north side of the attic was stacked with Liz's own belongings. She lifted the lid of a small blue tote and felt her strength ebb away like the tide.

His cards. Ray's.

Why would she punish herself by opening this? Perhaps to see if pain did diminish after months had passed, perhaps to see if she could summon enough courage to face the past. The card on top of the pile was an elaborate Christmas card, with embossed poinsettias and glittered gold ribbon.

TO MY DARLING.

The ensuing verse was filled with flowery prose, the declaration of a long and lasting love, the magical wonder of the season. His signature hurt most, the neat *R*, followed by a scribbled continuance. All a falsehood. A blatant lie. But she found herself riffling through the entire stack, the Valentine, the Easter card, the birthday card. She sighed, thinking of her own sincerity, her belief in his unwavering declaration of love. Did he know what love was? Did she?

She bit her lower lip, knowing suddenly that she had never felt the attraction to Ray that she now felt for Matthew. Another wave of shame rolled over her! This was what every Christian young girl was warned against, wasn't it? This weak-in-the-knees physical attraction? Wasn't it just sinful lust?

Well, either way, it wouldn't work out, so she better not let herself get carried away with silly feelings.

* * *

When the market van rolled in on Friday morning, she was wearing a new short-sleeved dress in aqua blue, her hair gleaming with a liberal amount of styling gel. She wore a spritz of fragrance.

Matthew did not say good morning the way he always did when she stepped up into the van, which caused her to double down on her efforts to put any notion of attraction out of her head and heart. There were a few mumbled hellos from the depths of cozy throws as market girls huddled in chilly vinyl seats. Liz found a seat and focused on not thinking about Matthew.

Arrival at market brought no attention from him, and Liz really did stop thinking about Sunday evening, instead pouring her energy into the task at hand. She turned on the grill and the oven, then flipped the switch to start the fan in the stainless steel hood, turned on the light above the grill. She cut potatoes, put sausage patties on the grill top, filled trays with bacon.

Annie brought her a mug of coffee and a cider doughnut, her favorite.

"Oh my. Thank you so much, Annie. You're a dear."

"I love these things." She took a large bite, closed her eyes and chewed gratefully. "They are so good."

Liz laughed, then noticed the white paper bag containing more of them. She raised her eyebrows.

"Don't worry, they're not all for me." Annie giggled like a school girl, then pushed the swinging doors and yelled, "*Kommet*! Doughnuts! *Kommet* on (Come on)!"

In came Ruthie, Priscilla, and Eva. When Liz saw Matthew enter, she quickly put down her coffee and turned back to the grill.

Liz listened to their friendly chatter as she flipped the sausages, turned the potatoes. Priscilla spoke loudly, saying things a bit inappropriate for someone her age, laughed harshly. Liz felt her stomach churn, thought again of the suspected liaison, something she had almost forgotten.

Matthew stayed quiet for the most part, ate his doughnut as Liz kept herself occupied by the grill.

"Boy, you're grouchy," Priscilla quipped loudly. "Hey, you!" she yelled in Liz's direction.

"Oh! Me? Sorry, didn't know you meant me. No, I'm not grouchy. Just busy."

"Alright, everybody out," Matthew said, shooing them out of the kitchen and then coming to stand close beside her. "Sorry," he said.

Liz looked up to find his eyes on hers, with an expression completely undecipherable. Instantly, the words she had been planning to say became imbedded in her throat, her knees weakened, and all common sense evaporated.

"It's . . . it's okay. No one bothered me."

"I know you have a lot of responsibility before we open, so I'll see it doesn't happen again, okay?"

"No, it's fine."

Because he was so close, her thoughts scattered like confetti. She could not think of a single phrase, her mind as rattled as an empty container, a sense of unease increasing by the second.

And still he stayed.

"I don't want to lose you."

He left immediately after that, and she literally had to grip the edge of the worktable to keep herself upright.

Oh my goodness, she breathed to herself.

* * *

The day flew by, the way all market days did for her. She moved efficiently from table to grill and back again, sending out orders for breakfast, then lunch. There were to-go orders put in Styrofoam boxes as well as orders plated on white stoneware plates. Annie was meticulous, arranging the ham or bacon just so, the toast cut in neat triangles, thick slices of homemade bread dripping with butter. Real butter, not spreadable margarine.

Liz was proud of the meals she made, felt capable and efficient. She appreciated Annie, her willingness to fill in when she needed a break, and was especially grateful after the dinner rush to collapse into a booth with a bowl of butternut squash soup.

She looked up to find Matthew watching her.

"Mind if I sit here?"

"No. Go ahead."

She gathered the farmhouse magazine, laid it on the seat beside her.

"What were you reading?"

"Oh, my sister Marianne is getting married," she said, holding up the magazine to show him. "She wants ideas for decorating around the farm. She'd love these yellow mums in this old galvanized bucket. See this?" He was staring at her, not the colorful cover. She blinked. "What?"

"You're so beautiful. How could someone spend a day on the grill and appear as fresh and pretty as you do?"

She stared at him. Her lips parted with a quick reply, but the sincerity in his eyes pushed it straight out of her mind. Words completely escaped her, but her eyes were held captive by the light in his.

"You know, Liz, I really enjoyed hanging out with you and Esther. I'd love to do something Saturday night."

Her heart was racing and her eyes had already betrayed her, but her good sense returned at the last second and she knew exactly what she needed to say.

"Matthew," she said quietly.

He strained to hear.

"I have been hurt. I'm sure you're used to girls running after you, but that's not me. It's going to take me a long time before I can trust again. I can't speak for Esther, so if she . . . if Henry is interested, I mean, go ahead without me."

Confused again suddenly, she pushed her spoon back and forth in her uneaten soup, her eyes lowered. When the silence crept on, she lifted bewildered eyes to find him watching her, his face like stone, the color having seeped out of it.

"You evidently know nothing about me." He said, still holding her gaze.

"No, no I don't."

"Trust me, Liz, I know how you feel."

"What do you mean?"

"Somewhere in the city of Baltimore, the love of my life is living as an English woman married to a divorced man. Why do you think I noticed Priscilla's situation so easily?"

"What?" Liz was completely shocked. Matthew had been heartbroken? Gorgeous, confident, perfect Matthew?

His nostrils flared with emotion. "It's four years now. She was the housecleaner for this wealthy couple and she fell in love. She knew it was wrong, and lived a double life for over a year. In the end, when I asked her to marry me, she confessed and left with him."

"Wow. I'm sorry."

"Don't be. God sees the whole picture. Just know you're not alone. You're not the only one who is scared to love again."

She stared at him for too long, taking it all in. He waited, just staring back. Later, when Liz thought back, she had no idea how much time passed like that. But something shifted in Liz's heart in those moments. She felt a warmth, a deep happiness, seeping through the cracks of her heart, and she couldn't have stopped it even if she'd wanted to.

"Okay. If we're in this together, let's just hang out for a while, see how it goes." She smiled genuinely.

"Thank you, Liz. Pick you up at seven?"

"And do what? Go where?"

"It's a surprise."

The remainder of the day was infused with a sort of golden light, and Liz moved through her tasks in a trance. Ruthie and Priscilla noticed the flushed cheeks, the spring in her step, and muttered teenaged jealousies under their breath. Annie was annoyed by their gossip and said firmly that Liz deserved a break, and if Matthew sat with her, they were likely discussing the ordering of supplies.

Chapter Four

"It's not a date, Esther."

Liz sat in the shop, her father's chair tilted at a dangerous angle, talking to her best friend on the phone. She listened patiently, wrapped the cord around a forefinger, then said. "Stop it."

She laughed.

"Henry? I don't know if he likes you or not. That's your job."

She smiled at Samuel when he came through the door, watched him searching through small bins of nuts, bolts, and screws.

"Alright, be that way. But if you don't want to go, then don't." She listened again, laughed, tried to say something, but realized the futility of it. "What am I wearing? I don't know yet."

Esther was being difficult, something Liz had not bargained for. She thought it was too soon to be going out with them, but after a lengthy discussion, she agreed to give it a shot. It was so much like

Esther. She said she wanted to be in a relationship, but there was never a guy quite good enough in her opinion. She always found some shortcoming. She thought Henry was a little too short and not too bright.

Henry, in Liz's opinion, was quite a catch for Esther, with her buck teeth and blunt manner.

She ran into the house after her phone conversation, her slippers wet from the cold dew already settling on the grass.

"Hard frost in the morning," her father said from behind the daily paper.

"Really?" her mother asked, then launched into colorful phrases of gratitude, so glad some old traditions had gone out the window, such as growing your own celery for a wedding. "Now, just imagine, Elmer. We'd have to be out there covering all those rows of celery. What a pain. Same as chopping off the heads of all those fat hens. Absolutely not. Just have them delivered."

"Well," her father began, then lowered the paper to get his wife's attention. "Back then, they didn't invite four hundred guests, either. Two hundred was a big wedding. It should still be that way. These huge weddings are out of control."

"Ach now, Elmer. You never were one for weddings. Don't let Marianne hear you."

Her father reached for another graham cracker, dipped it in milk, and swallowed it quickly, savored the flavor of peanut butter, cracker, and milk.

"I'll be glad when it's over. Thanksgiving and Christmas, too." Mam turned to Liz. "Well, at least we don't have to worry about Liz marrying anyone anytime soon, *gel* (right), Liz?"

"Nope," she quipped, then took the stairs two at a time, on her way to fling herself on her recliner before staring happily into gold-dusted space.

* * *

All day Saturday, work went well, excitement doubling her energy. Annie regaled her with stories of her new arch supports and how her feet felt so much better today. She moved around the kitchen like a great barge, her small arch-supported feet propelling her quite efficiently, her wide girth even wider today, in an astonishing shade of magenta, a pinkish red dress that was seriously much too short, giving her the appearance of a gleaming Easter egg.

Liz had no idea how she'd managed without her and never took her efforts for granted.

Priscilla was evasive, sneaking in and out of the kitchen like a nervous cat, so Matthew followed her when she left the restaurant to stroll the aisles of the farmer's market without asking for her break. Liz watched all this as she wiped down tables, set the salt and pepper shakers on the counter to be filled. She told Ruthie to be more careful watching the amount of napkins in the dispensers, which made her toss her head in an irritated way.

"Come on, Ruthie. I don't mean to be rude, but this is the waitress's job. If you would see to it in the morning, it wouldn't be a problem."

"Okay, whatever."

Liz walked away, holding her tongue. Seriously, these young girls were so spoiled, so headstrong. Was she old and grumpy, or were girls different than they used to be? Perhaps a bit of both.

When Matthew returned, he had a glowering Priscilla in tow, his face stern and uncompromising. Liz stayed away, knowing if there was anything to relate, he'd tell her this evening.

This evening. Was any of this actually happening? It all felt pretty surreal. But she kept an even keel with a businesslike manner, a brisk sense of getting her job done while listening to Annie's tales, stories, and opinions.

"You know, Liz, I said to Elam the other day, remember when dating was *schemmich* (shameful)? The young fellows used to sneak around to the girl's house. It was nothing new for a young man to date a girl for a few years and rarely meet up with her parents. Well, not so much in my day, as the way my mother would describe it. Times change. Now, the dating fellow sits with the family to eat, or they go along on vacation. Our Daniel went to the Great Smokey Mountains with his girl last summer. Boy, I wasn't happy. Too much time together. They'll get into *dummhelta* (stupidity). You know how it goes with young people. I'll tell you one thing, it's no wonder these two (jerking her thumb toward the dining area) aren't dating. Grouchy, spoiled little things. Excuse me, but if I was Matthew, I'd fire Priscilla. I think he should.

"Is your mam ready for the wedding? I guess not, huh? What is it, two more weeks? Three? Oh *hesslich* (seriously), I'm glad I'm not her. Making a wedding drives me straight over the edge, but then, Elam isn't a big help like some men are. He's too easygoing, thinking *Voss shots? Voss shots?* (What does it matter?) Well, things matter. You can't have wedding guests all dressed up coming into a sloppy area with dusty benches and carpets that aren't cleaned right. Oh, I tell you, our neighbors, Check's Sal's Abe's Amos, they had a wedding . . ."

At the mention of four names in a row, Liz's eyes went out of focus, her ears no longer hearing what Annie was saying, but she smiled and nodded her head at regular intervals, which seemed perfectly sufficient. She looked around the kitchen with satisfaction, turned off the lights and the fans, then let herself out. The dining room floor had been mopped, the chairs upended on the tables, and Matthew was closing up.

"Thanks, girls. I appreciate your work. Did you get your tip from the jar?"

Never had a ride home seemed longer. Liz knew she would have less than two hours to get ready for the evening, and she had not told her parents or her sisters. They'd be more than a little surprised.

* * *

When seven o'clock arrived, he was there with a driver, a white mini van with Henry and Esther in the back seat, Matthew stepping out to allow her to get in first. She knew her shocked parents were peering out of windows, and she played it for all it was worth, taking her time getting into the van. She was perplexed when Matthew walked toward the house with a note in his hand, knocked on the door, and handed it to her parents—who, she could tell by the look on their faces, were even more perplexed.

"What was that?" She asked as he slipped into the car beside her.

"Just letting them know where we're headed. It's a surprise for you, but I don't want them to worry.

I know you're an adult, but they don't know us . . . and we might be back later than they're expecting." He and Henry exchanged glances with a little smile.

Liz smiled too, though the whole thing was a little odd. So thoughtful, though—so respectful to consider her parents' concerns.

It seemed so long since she'd done anything even close to this, and she felt special, blessed. She could feel his eyes on her face, which was hugely flattering, but she downplayed his attention, aware of Esther's reluctance in the back seat.

"Ok, now Liz is in the car. You can tell us where we're going." Esther didn't ask. She ordered.

"You'll see," Matthew assured her.

Henry smiled at Esther, and Liz felt a stab of empathy. She knew Esther intimidated him, could tell he was being quiet, afraid of saying or doing the wrong thing, and to her, this brought a feeling of outrage against her best friend, which she kept tamped down successfully.

They drove south, then turned into a narrow dirt road, away from the traffic, the lights, and the excitement of restaurants, business, people coming and going. Liz noticed the driver's smile, looked questioningly at Matthew, but he was staring straight ahead and would not meet her eye.

Esther could not hide her indignation. "Come on, guys. What in the world?"

Henry burst out laughing, and Liz caught Esther's exasperated look.

"Are we going to eat? I'm actually really hungry."

"Oh, you'll eat, Esther. Don't worry."

"What? Acorns and wild cabbage?"

It was getting dark, the light being snuffed out far too quickly, the beautiful fall colors slowly losing their brilliance. When the road turned uphill, winding between trees and alongside a steep ridge, the ground falling away in a stomach-churning ascent, Liz could not keep from gasping.

Matthew's hand touched her sleeve, then grasped her hand firmly, his long fingers wrapping comfortably around hers. She looked at him, but in the near darkness, found his expression hidden.

"Really now," Esther lamented. "What is this? An abduction? You are kidnapping us, aren't you?"

Henry chortled, but didn't exactly answer. The driver seemed to be in on the secret, grinning, talking to Matthew about anything except the steep, winding dirt road.

Suddenly in the half light of evening, the woods fell away to a clearing, with the golden glow of two porch lights beside a wide front door, a front porch that undoubtedly boasted a panoramic view of the surrounding countryside.

When the van stopped, the driver swiveled around and said, "Have a great weekend, gals!"

Both of them were speechless as they emerged, standing in awe as they realized the size and authenticity of a real mountain cabin.

"Here we are," Matthew announced, squeezing her hand before he let go of it.

"Where exactly are we?" Esther said turning slowly in a circle.

"See you Sunday night," Matthew told the driver.

"Sunday night? Tomorrow? We're staying overnight? What?" This from Esther, who was obviously having a fit.

Liz couldn't blame her. This was a little crazy. "You're teasing, right?" She half smiled at Matthew.

"Do you want me to be?"

Matthew stood close, looking down into her face, and Liz had no idea what to say. Was this even real life? Now she understood why he'd given the note to her parents. What on earth would they think?

"Listen," he said, turning to include Esther. "Let's just have dinner and then see what we feel like. Believe it or not, there are neighbors beyond the trees over there and they have a phone. If you want a ride back this evening, that's totally fine. But the sunrise here is incredible."

"Tooth brush. Pajamas." Esther, always practical, was clearly trying to wrap her head around their situation. "We have nothing."

"We took care of all that," Matthew said, as he led the way up to the massive steps leading to the front porch. The post-and-beam construction was amazing, heavy planks forming wide steps and a deep front porch with the same flooring. Rustic Adirondack chairs were placed at specific points to allow the viewer a grand spectacle of the mountains surrounding them. There were potted ferns, with colorful mums and deep purple asters placed in a colorful array. The front door was especially beautiful, constructed of oak boards, with a beveled glass window, side windows reaching from floor to ceiling.

"Wow. Oh my!" Liz breathed.

"Alright. I know you don't own this," Esther began, in her no-nonsense way.

"Actually," Matthew began.

Liz caught Henry placing a forefinger to his lips, his eyebrows drawn down in a warning.

Matthew fumbled his words, tried changing the subject.

Esther was quick to catch the denial, swiveled to meet Henry's gaze. "The truth now. You'll be caught if you're *schnitzing*."

Matthew and Henry looked at each other, shrugged their shoulders.

Esther would have none of it, kept up her senseless badgering for the full truth until Liz told her to let it go. Did it really matter?

The interior was breathtaking, with log walls, pine flooring, and a solid wall of windows opening to the west, where streaks of purple and orange lay like strips of ragged fabric on a dark gray background. Lights were dimmed, casting a cozy glow across comfortable leather sofas, deep armchairs, and ottomans. A huge stone fireplace took up most of the space between the massive windows.

The kitchen was behind a half wall, complete with a full wall of pine cabinets, a kitchen island with bar stools surrounding it, a stacked refrigerator, and beautiful stainless steel gas stove. Henry went to the fridge and started taking things out while Matthew led the girls up the stairs.

The open stairway led to a loft on the second floor, where three bedrooms and a full bath took up the space. There were comfortable beds piled with pillows, tasteful quilts, and extra throws, dressers with mirrors and full closets.

Behind her, Matthew said softly, "My sisters keep um . . . whatever you'll need up here."

"Can't you say nighties and underwear?" Esther quipped.

Matthew tried to stay cool, but he turned a shade of red, became flustered, and went downstairs. Liz found this endearing, respectful somehow.

Sometimes, as she grew older, she realized the morals among the youth were deteriorating at an alarming rate, which made her feel old and sour, disapproving. It was an emotion she did not like, brought another longing for her past to have turned out differently. She could be married now, living in her own cozy home with Ray, the one man she had truly loved. She felt the need for parents to come to grips with the dangers of the world slipping unobserved into the culture of the *rumschpringa*, something that had always been there, but seemed to be especially prevalent with the introduction of cellphones.

Esther giggled behind her raised hand. Liz couldn't help laughing.

"Poor thing," Esther said.

"I think it's cute. Very respectful," Liz said.

"You're already gone on him," Esther observed.

"No. No, I'm not."

"Say what you want. You are." Esther waved a hand airily. "Do you think Henry really owns this place? Whatever!" she whispered in a subdued shriek.

"Would help, huh?" Liz elbowed her, which brought on a quick yelp.

Henry looked up from the living room. "Everything okay up there?"

"Don't worry about us, okay?"

Matthew was already in the kitchen, pulling pans off a rack that hung from the ceiling near the stove. Liz and Esther joined the guys and they all worked together to produce a wonderful meal of strip steak, peppers, onion, zucchini, and mushrooms. Esther made a salad of fresh lettuce, avocado, walnuts, and cranberries, with bottled dressing. A loaf of whole wheat bread with softened butter and raspberry jam rounded out the meal. Afterward, they took their coffee to the front porch, snuggled into heavy woolen throws, and watched the full moon sail among the myriad twinkling stars. And they talked.

They talked about serious matters, discussed the world at large, the future of the Amish church, the people who could no longer give up to the *ordnung,* the horses and buggies as a way of transportation, the horse often standing in the pasture for weeks on end as drivers were hired to take groups from place to place. Things were not the same as they had been a century ago. Change came slowly, but relentlessly.

Henry proved to be a brilliant conversationalist.

"Yeah, my mother says she remembers her uncles sitting around discussing buying and selling, how there was no way there would ever be an Amish storeowner. It simply wouldn't be allowed, not ever."

"Oh my goodness," Esther breathed.

"My mother is in her seventies, and this was back when she was a child."

"How old are you?" Esther asked.

"Ancient. I'm old. Gray hair, arthritic limbs," Henry chuckled. "No, my mother was forty-two when I was born. So that makes me, what? Twenty-seven next month."

"Old," Esther said firmly. She looked at him under the yellow glow of the porch light. "How come you never married?" she asked, straightforward as always.

There was a long pause.

"Don't tell me you had your heart broken like Liz."

"No, nothing like that. Just never found the right one, I suppose."

"You're picky."

"Maybe."

"So what do you do for a living?"

"I build things."

"What kind of things?"

He waved a hand. "This. Log homes."

"You built this?"

"Yes. Matthew and I."

"You're kidding me."

"No."

When Esther stayed quiet, Liz grinned. *Aha*, she thought. *Gotcha*. For once in her life, Esther had no response to Henry's quiet "no." Liz felt he was truly humble, and this was the reason Esther remained quiet.

Liz shivered, the night air heavy with dew settling around her exposed shoulders, the throw having slipped down her arms.

"Chilly," she said and got to her feet. "And it must be getting late. Are we . . ." She trailed off, the thought of heading home that night suddenly disappointing. But what about Esther? She didn't want her friend to feel pressured into staying.

"Eh, let's stay," Esther announced bluntly, seeming to read her thoughts. "There's no way I'm riding back down that crazy road in the dark."

So that settled it. They were spending the night. It was an unusual first date, but then, none of them were kids. They wouldn't fall into the same kinds of temptations youth sometimes do, and Henry and Matthew were clearly God-fearing men. Her parents would raise their eyebrows questioningly when she returned home, but they wouldn't question her choice out loud. Such things were kept private.

Liz turned to sink back down in her chair.

"Come sit with me," Matthew said, opening his arms. Clad in a warm sweatshirt, he looked perfectly comfortable. Liz eyed him with disbelief.

"Um . . . I . . . I'm okay. Just need to adjust my blanket."

"There's room, Liz. It's only going to get colder out here."

Her heart was thudding heavily in her chest, so that she was afraid he would hear it if she sat too close to him. She knew, too, she wanted to sit there more than she had ever wanted to do anything. But if she did so, would she be flinging herself off the side of a cliff, to fall headlong into serious injuries of the heart?

What about the pain of being rebuffed, of being told you are not good enough, that you wore his love long enough, and it had been replaced? Nothing could ever take away the memory of his words, every syllable like a dagger, hurting, hurting. How could she ever be stupid enough to risk it a second time?

Her feet had a mind of their own, however, and she found herself being pulled by a strange magnetic force, until she was seated beside him. His arm was a solid comfort, wrapped around her shoulders. As the conversation resumed, she released against him, the good, solid strength of him. When he spoke, she could feel the side of his chest rising and falling, hear the intake of breath.

And Henry, bless his heart, did exactly the right thing. He remained aloof, chatting comfortably, letting Esther take the lead.

It was very late when the men wished the girls a good night and retired to their own bedroom, leaving

Liz and Esther to their showers and shared bed, where they whispered and giggled like schoolgirls.

Esther said in a sorrowful voice, "Henry certainly didn't want me sitting with him."

"You just met him. He's a smart man."

"I know. Wow." There was a pause before she asked, "Liz, you seriously think he owns this place?"

* * *

The morning brought overcast skies, gray clouds roiling restlessly overhead, the warm glow of the shaded lamps even cozier. Henry started a log fire in the fireplace to take the chill off, and Matthew asked Liz if she'd mind making breakfast while he brought in more wood, seeing how she was used to the grill at market.

Everything was delicious, the mountain air giving them a good appetite, after which they hiked the trails surrounding the cabin, weaving among the dense stands of deciduous trees, dark green firs, and thorny underbrush. They visited the spring, then came to a lake called Torey Pond, complete with flocks of ducks and migrating geese. They experienced the sight of a huge buck and a few does, stepping cautiously from the surrounding forest, delicately bending their heads to drink from the cold waters of the lake.

On the way home, Henry and Esther walked ahead, and Liz found herself walking in comfortable silence with Matthew. He walked slowly, as if to lengthen the amount of time they would spend together, and she found herself wishing they had many more miles to the cabin.

"You know, Liz, you're one of the few girls I've ever been with who realizes the value of being comfortable with silence."

Liz looked up at him, found his eyes directly on hers. They shared a long look of mutual admiration, until Liz smiled.

"I don't always know what to say."

"And that is such a great quality."

"Thank you."

"Do you realize how much I want to know you better?"

She shook her head.

"I do. I want to spend every weekend with you, Liz. Can we try? See if it works out?"

His eyes remained steadily on hers, the flicker of light intensifying as they stood beneath the dull clouds, the canopy of decaying leaves casting an even darker shadow.

She was bereft of words, the weight of past heartaches pushing against the courage to say yes. Undecided, she opened her mouth to say no, but the refusal remained stuck in her throat.

"I . . ." she began.

He stepped closer. "It's okay. Take your time."

She swallowed hard, was terrified to find tears springing to the surface. He would find her a terrible coward, a cringing person afraid of her own shadow. *Oh God,* she thought wildly, *tell me now, which path should I take? I want to trust him, but how can I?*

"It's just that . . ."

And then tears did spill from her eyes. Her lower lip trembled, so she caught it quickly between her teeth. She stepped back, turned away, so he would not notice her cowardice. She stood alone, her back turned toward him, her hands shoved in the pocket of her sweatshirt. The gray forest was completely still, except for the rattling of an acorn falling through branches, bringing a few crisp leaves from their precarious hold on decaying stems.

She heard the rustling of leaves as he approached her, blinked furiously to rid herself of unwanted tears. Her shoulders stiffened as she felt his fingers wrap around her forearms.

"Liz."

When there was no response, he turned her slowly, gently, until she was almost against him.

"Look at me, Liz."

She refused. Her long, thick lashes swept her cheeks as the tears clung there, slowly made their way down across them.

"Liz, I'm serious. Look . . ."

With a cry of broken despair, she tore out of his grasp and began to run, blindly, putting all the distance between them she possibly could, her thoughts in a wild jumble of mistrust, self-loathing, captive to the wrenching horror of being jilted a month before the beginning of her life with Ray. She had loved, had trusted blindly, like a child, had been led unwillingly to suffer every young girl's nightmare. As she ran, the buzzing swarm of fear and doubt, refusal to trust another man, low self-worth, and tortured despair following her efficiently.

Chapter Five

THE REMAINDER OF THE DAY WAS MADE UP OF a desperate stab at normalcy, but all of them knew the life of the weekend had gone up in smoke. Matthew kept up the usual banter for the sake of his friends, and Liz retreated to a quiet space no one could fully understand.

The white van's appearance was a mercy, the ride home the perfect example of a false façade, an appearance of happiness and appreciation with a lifeless core.

On Monday, she gave him her one week's notice. She ignored the look of pain in his eyes, told him he hadn't done anything wrong. She just couldn't pretend she would ever be ready for a relationship, and it wasn't fair to him to string him along. And though she didn't say it out loud, she knew it wasn't fair to herself to keep hanging around his gorgeous eyes and arms and everything else when she would never be able to trust him. It would be torture for both of them. He tried to apologize, said he shouldn't have taken her to the cabin so soon, that it was too much, but she waved it off. "It's just better that we part ways now, before . . ."

"Before what?" He looked at her with those aching eyes.

She didn't answer, but instead left his office, returning to the kitchen.

She worked mechanically, trained Annie to be the grill cook, did her best to keep from noticing Matthew. She turned her eyes away from Matthew in a yellow polo shirt, his muscles straining as he lifted fifty-pound bags of flour. She refused to keep glancing at Matthew in a sky blue button-down, talking earnestly to Priscilla, who tossed her head and marched away, a dark cloud of anger over her face.

Truthfully, she knew where he was every minute of every day, until the last Saturday evening and her final ride in the market van. Annie was still not aware of Liz's reason for quitting her job so abruptly, but she wisely kept most of her opinions to herself, choosing to appreciate the fact she'd get a chance at cooking. She was pretty sure she could do better than

Liz, who had a tendency to undercook her eggs. You had to be careful with things like that.

* * *

With her job gone, her parents bewildered, and her life once again in upheaval, the date of her sister's wedding could not have come at a worse time. Liz worked at home, getting up at the crack of dawn and throwing herself into the job at hand, which was to groom the entire farm with a fine-toothed comb.

The lawn and garden were meticulously mowed, trimmed, tilled, and edged. Fresh mulch was scattered over the shrubs and flowerbeds, white chrysanthemums placed in every one. Marianne was a sparkling bundle of nerves, her adrenaline fueled as she ran from one duty to another, her groom-to-be working tirelessly to clean the barn, lay the carpet in the huge pole building, every task done willingly.

Liz persuaded herself she had done the right thing. Matthew could talk as eloquently as he pleased about his own shattered hopes and dreams, but he was too handsome, too suave, and exactly the kind of guy that sent girls down a dangerous path. Give them a handsome young man and stars appeared where common sense should be. Off they went, whisked away to some dreamscape of their own, only to drop out of that unstable cloud and land with a thud on their backside.

She had traveled that route before, only Matthew was far more handsome than Roy. Probably smarter, humbler, and more successful, too. What a combo. Good thing she escaped while she still could.

Her head was held high on the *risht daug* (day of preparation). Teased by the many uncles and aunts about being the older one and allowing her sister to marry out of turn, she took it in stride quite gallantly, she thought, thinking of quick comebacks with a wide smile and a proud toss of her head.

The interior of the large shed was transformed into a wedding place, with long rows of gleaming pine benches, rows of folding chairs for the ministers and older relatives. A makeshift kitchen, complete with five gas stoves, numerous folding tables, large dishpans to do dishes, shelf after shelf containing empty serving dishes, baskets, napkins, all the ingredients needed to cook two large meals for more than four hundred guests.

There was a room for the *eck leit* (corner people), the four young couples chosen to be the servers of the bridal party seated around the corner, where the long length of tables met. Hidden away were the bride's tablecloth, china, silverware, stemware, all of it washed and polished the day before by the *eck leit*, the sight of it a surprise to the bride and groom as they were seated after the service.

* * *

The day was perfect, crisp and cold in the morning, sunny and gently warm. Liz was in the bridal party, being a sister to the bride, seated beside one of the groom's cousins, a tall, lanky young man with a bored expression, his hair barely meeting the standards of an Amish haircut. At sixteen years old, many of the *rumschpringa* went to a barber, had their hair cut in the way of the English, and went about the start of their time with the youth in a fashionable way, much to the varied approval or disapproval of their parents. But asked to be a *nāva hucka* (a common label for those in the bridal party) meant the boys must let their hair grow back into the *ordnung* of the Amish. Anxious mothers watched every inch as it slowly grew into a semblance of the correct length.

His name was Joel, and without a doubt he was less than thrilled to spend an entire day with Liz. She was old, he'd heard, although she wasn't bad looking. She was definitely not cool. He had eyes only for Emmaline King, the seventeen-year-old who he had invited for *nāva sitz buddy*. He'd been allowed to invite two, so one had been her and the other his closest buddy, Aaron Jay.

The wedding went off without any major problem, directed and run smoothly by capable relatives well-versed in the way of quietly and decorously seating more than four hundred people. First, they seated the parents and grandparents, aunts and uncles, followed by coworkers and bosses, who ranked quite high in the line-up. After that were friends of the family, cousins, followed by the long lines of the youth.

The service was more than three hours, with the many workers in the background doing the allotted duties. There were the *roasht leid*, the four couples chosen to make the mountain of *roasht*, a chicken filling made with bread cubes, butter, eggs, celery, and whole chickens cut into bite-sized pieces after being roasted. *Die 'grumbare leit* were the three young couples chosen to peel, boil, and mash over a hundred pounds of potatoes, complete with copious amounts of butter, cream cheese, heated milk, and salt. At every stove, the older ladies were given their job of making gravy or cooking the great kettles of cut celery into the favorite dish called simply *ga-cucheda tzellrich* (cooked celery). Flavored with evaporated milk, brown sugar, vinegar, and salt, thickened with a white sauce, it was an old traditional dish that went well with *roasht* and mashed potatoes. In another area of the kitchen, young women were grouped around plastic tables, armed with graters as they shoved quartered heads of cabbage up and down, up and down, turning them into pepper slaw. Older women hovered and fussed like biddy hens after the addition of salt, sugar, and vinegar, tasting repeatedly, heads shaking. Too much vinegar, not enough sugar.

As the long service drew to a close, a delicious aroma swirled among the seated guests, whetting appetites, everyone eager for the service to come to an end. A hush fell over the entire shed as the minister came to the part where Sarah was given in marriage to Tobias, an old story from the Apocrypha, the form used to unite the Amish couple in holy matrimony. They were given in marriage by the solemn vows of the bishop, their almost whispered "Ya" a sacred occasion. When they returned to their seats, the scramble to begin the final preparations began, the long prayer and last joyous hymn marking the end of the ceremony.

Doughnuts and cookies were put on fancy plates, tapioca pudding scooped into pretty bowls, jam, butter and rolls, coleslaw, and applesauce ready to be whisked out to the vast amount of benches turned magically into tables. The minute the great room was emptied, the men appeared and began the work of setting the benches on extensions, forming row after row of tables. Women appeared with rolls of plastic tablecloths, with layers of white paper towels on which the plates would be set, the towels a necessity with repeated settings. It was all organized, each person taking their duty seriously, and so being able to keep *da hochztich* day tradition alive and well.

* * *

She couldn't understand why Matthew was there. She was seated with the bridal party beside Joel, her white cape and apron immaculate, starched and brand new, covering the navy blue of her dress, a black covering on her head. The black signified an unmarried girl, whereas a white covering meant a married woman. The black covering was worn only to church, with the white cape and apron. In the afternoon, after Marianne was married, they changed her black covering to a white one.

She'd felt the color drain from her face when she noticed him. One of the first of the young men to be seated, there was no mistaking the handsome face, the perfect haircut, his wide shoulders and comfortable stance. But only for a moment she felt the fluttering of her pulse, the weakness in her knees, before she felt determined calm return. She would be fine. He meant nothing to her.

She had removed herself quite efficiently from any frightening entanglement with a young man who was far too handsome and much too sure of himself. It had been foolish to go on a date with him at all, especially foolish to spend the night and allow her heart to begin attaching to his. But with prayer and sacrifice, anything could be overcome.

Anything.

She kept her eyes lowered with respect, resented Joel's fidgeting, wished he'd get that wad of chewing gum out of his mouth. It was embarrassing, too, the way he stretched out his skinny legs and tugged at his trousers, just above the knees. As if she hadn't already spied his thin, bony ankles plenty of times.

As the great swelling tune of the last song reached a crescendo, she looked out across the guests and felt a stab of electricity as she looked directly into Matthew Zook's fervent gaze. Immediately, her eyelids lowered, only to be released as if on springs, to find his eyes on her face, imploring her, raising uncomfortable questions.

Why, Liz? Why? Why did you do this to me?

His eyes contained bewilderment, and a sadness that wrenched at her heart. She steeled herself, erected her defenses immediately.

No, I won't do this, Matthew.

And in the evening, by all that could possibly be unlucky, she found herself seated across from him, he having been chosen to escort the *nāva sitz buddy* to the table for the evening meal, an old custom, the young men paired with the single girls to sit beside each other for the meal and the hymn singing afterward.

Directly across from him.

Her mind refused to accepts this, even as she said hello. His girl was none other than Ella Stoltzfus, a beautiful, blue-eyed blond sought after by most of the young men she knew. A perfect match. More power to both of them. Her scalloped potatoes stuck in her throat as she watched him turn his face to speak to her, attentive, charming. Ella gave a high musical laugh, and he flashed his perfect, white smile. Liz choked, quickly raised her water glass to her lips, seriously contemplating sliding down off her chair, crawling beneath the table, and disappearing completely.

The food on her plate turned into an inedible mass, and when Joel asked her why she wasn't eating, she told him she ate all afternoon, why did she have to? He was so busy flirting with the gregarious Emmaline, he didn't hear what she said anyway, so she sat in misery, taking sips of water and trying to keep her eyes off Matthew and Ella.

When Ella was occupied, talking to the person on her right, she heard her name called very softly. She set down her water glass, raised stricken eyes to Matthew's searching ones.

"Can I talk to you this evening?" he asked quickly.

She shook her head, lowered her eyes.

But there he was, as she made her way to the house after most of the guests had begun to leave, a starry-eyed Marianne and her new husband relaxing, thanking relatives, basking in the glow of their successful blessed day and each other.

"Liz, please. Can we talk?"

He was certainly persistent.

"What is there to say?"

"I miss you at work."

"Really."

"Eva quit. Priscila is still acting strangely. I need you to come back."

"I can't, Matthew."

"Why not?"

"Because I just can't, that's all."

"Just to work, Liz. It doesn't have to be anything more than that. I thought you loved the market."

She shook her head.

All around them, wedding guests moved away into waiting vans, unruly horses pawing the ground, waiting till the wife or girlfriend appeared. Children bounded through the dark like rabbits, fueled by a steady diet of candy and doughnuts, cookies and punch. Everywhere, the darkness was filled with movement, chaos, just the way her mind was spinning, searching for answers.

"Matthew."

"What?"

He stepped closer. She backed away but found herself against the gate to the horse pasture.

"It's too risky."

"It doesn't have to be. You've worked there for years. It can just be the way it was before . . . before I messed it up."

She opened her mouth, then closed it, made a quick move to get away, but he caught her arm just as swiftly, drew her even closer and said in a harsh, gravelly voice tense with emotion, "Look. I hate my restaurant without you. There's no point. I'm selling out. I'm tired of dealing with everything."

"You can't do that."

"I'm going to."

"You're just doing it to make me feel guilty."

"No, no. Liz, it's not what I meant. I just miss you, and everything is . . . I don't know how to say it."

She made another move to go. He kept his hand on her arm.

"Why is it too risky? You mean me?"

In a small voice, so low it was no more than a whisper, she said, "Yes."

"You mean you can't trust me?"

"Yes."

His great laugh rang out, joyous, uncontained. A few bustling women in shawls and bonnets hurried past, their faces outlined against their black bonnets, thinking how bold these *rumschpringa* were these days.

Now she'd gone and done it. Threw herself right off the same cliff without a parachute.

"Well, let me be totally transparent then. I do really need you as an employee, and I meant what I said about things being the way they were before if that's what you really want. But I also still have feelings for you. I watched you sitting there today, and I realized I have to give it everything I've got." He paused, searching her eyes. "Maybe you'd better learn to trust God, Liz. I'm serious." He took his hand away from her arm and put it to her waist, as gently and lightly as a benediction. "Why don't we decide to seek the Lord's counsel? Why don't we both take this very seriously, in a spiritual way, make God the One who decides? I think perhaps we both need a hefty dose of faith, a renewal of our minds. When the minister came across the part where Sarah had seven husbands who died on their wedding night, and Tobias went right ahead with his faith in God, I realized what is missing."

Everything shifted then. He had spoken truth and she could not escape it. It had cut her to the core, but not in a painful way—more like a beam of light piercing through to her heart.

She lifted her hand so hesitantly, then placed it against his side. She felt the fabric of his vest, where the satin back met the black polyester of the front, felt the seam where it had been pressed. She was close, but not close enough. His vest was open, so she lifted the opposite hand and very lightly placed it gently between the opened vest and the softness of his white shirt. She looked up at him by the dim light of the moving buggies. She heard him draw a deep breath.

"You're right. I'm not ready to come back to market yet, but I will pray about it. Thank you. I . . . I think I needed to hear that."

And so began the time she could only describe as joyous. All was not lost, not at all, neither was anything promised. The realization that nothing is ever promised, but the fact that we live by faith was the most astounding thing. The weak, earthly assurance she tried to give herself was positively void. She found that the more she sought the face of God, the more she spent time with His Word, the more time she spent on her knees in prayer, the greater her horizons opened.

She helped Marianne settle into her new home and, with a love she didn't know she was capable of, hugged her and wished her a genuine blessing for years to come.

Henry and Esther began dating, a fact she never let Liz forget, repeatedly going over every detail of their time together, followed by how kind he was, how well mannered, how much money he had, and the clincher, he was taking her to the cabin for the first day of deer season.

"Alone," she quipped.

Liz slanted her a look. "You sure that's a good idea?"

"Pooh. You and your immoral thoughts. Henry is a perfect gentleman. Hasn't even held my hand."

Liz raised an eyebrow. "You serious?"

"Nope. And we won't touch each other, either."

"Good. Good for you." Even as she said that, she thought that as long as she lived, she would remember the touch of Matthew's soft white shirt, the sound of his breath, not to mention the comfort of resting against his strong arm in the Adirondack chair that night. Oh, the beauty of what God had designed for two consenting souls. The Scripture was full of the wonders of love of a man for a woman. She'd allow Esther her sanctimonious attitude, see what happened after deer season.

"Whatever went wrong for you and Matthew? He was all lovey that first night we were at the cabin."

"Yeah, he was."

"So why can't I get anything out of you?"

"Because."

"Look, we have never kept anything from each other, ever. Why now?"

"It's serious business, you know that. We decided to pray about it, try and exercise more faith in God and less in ourselves. I can't do anything about my fear of being hurt, except take it to God."

"Wow. That's deep."

"It is."

* * *

As fall turned colder, the last of the brittle leaves fell from the cold, dark branches. Thanksgiving came on the wings of a cold hard rain that was driven by a harsh, battering wind rattling around the corners of the farmhouse, sending shivers up Liz's back as she left her bedroom. She wore a bathrobe and her hair tied back in a ponytail. She could feel the heat of the kitchen before she entered. Mam was already hard at work preparing the turkey for the oven. It was a little past five in the morning, and Liz could tell by the way Mam moved that her hip was bothering her. She often talked about how they needed to buy a king-sized bed, with all her aches and pains and no place to stretch out that hip once it got to hurting. Elmer was a big man, and when they both occupied the queen-sized mattress, it was a *schmottz* (pain).

Mam looked up and smiled, grabbed another handful of stuffing, that savory mixture of celery, onion, broth, and sausage, and shoved it into the cavity, then another.

"Thought you might need some help, Mam."

"Why, that's really nice of you. I appreciate it."

Mam slid the turkey into the oven and then moved to the sink to wash her hands.

"I think we have time for a cup of coffee first."

Liz smiled, "You're addicted, Mam."

"But it's a good addiction. Coffee is good for you now."

Liz nodded, watched her mother lift the coffee pot and pour the boiling water over the Folgers in the filter, then set it back on the stove.

Liz stretched and yawned. "Who's all coming today?"

"Doddy, Mommy, Uncle Dans, Mark, and Marianne."

"Marianne and Mark are so happy," Liz said wistfully.

"Yes, they seem to be."

A comfortable silence fell across the room as the smell of fresh brewed coffee swirled between them. The wind moaned in the eaves, the rain shushing against the north window panes.

Liz shivered.

"So when will your turn come?" Mam asked, her voice belying her concern that her beloved daughter, the light of her life, was destined for spinsterhood.

"Turn for what?"

"Being married."

"Mam, you know what? There is no hurry. I'm not worried. I'm in a really good place right now. Things will happen as God wants them to. Some girls get married at thirty."

"Maybe so, but then it's usually some widower with a bunch of kids, and everyone acts likes she's so blessed to have found the man. Meanwhile, the poor unsuspecting girl has no idea what she's in for."

Liz looked shocked, her eyes opening wide. "Mam! Really?"

Mam thumped the coffeepot to hurry it up a bit, then bent to retrieve her beloved French vanilla creamer from the refrigerator.

"I struggle with that, Liz. I do. I want better for you."

"I'm sure there is a special blessing for those who undertake a journey like that."

"Don't you go kidding yourself now. You would never survive."

Liz silently rocked with laughter.

"Whatever happened to that Matthew? He was at the wedding. Dat said someone saw you talking to him afterward. Isn't Esther dating now?"

"Yes."

Mam sighed, sipped her coffee. "I wish you would be."

Then she told her mother about how she and Matthew had decided to pray about a future together, which lifted Mam's spirits to the extent that she sent Suzanna to the phone to call old Davey and Mary Beiler, just in case they had nothing going over the holidays. She got chills, thinking of Matthew and Liz, which escalated her spirits even more. The rain lashed the house with its fury, but the turkey turned out perfectly, the skin crispy and golden brown, the stuffing savory, fluffy, and succulent. The gravy was the best she'd ever made.

Liz basked in the coziness of their home, her mam's happiness, the pleasures of good food and laughter and family. She thought of Matthew often, wondered what he was doing for Thanksgiving, imagined him at the table with her. But mostly she enjoyed the warm feeling in her heart and the peace that had settled over her mind ever since she'd committed herself to trusting God's path for her life, whatever that turned out to be.

Chapter Six

SHE WENT BACK TO WORK.

The week after Thanksgiving was a slow time, but only for the one weekend, before Christmas shoppers created a throng of people dressed in the holiday reds, greens, and occasional dots of silver or gold. Decorations were hung at every vendor's stand and free candy canes appeared in dishes or hung from greenery that embellished the brick walls.

Liz was happy to be back. Orders flooded the kitchen and she picked up the pace accordingly, enjoying the hustle. And Annie was happy to have her back. She knew there was no way she could have kept up with the crowds on her own. Matthew was fully occupied with his own duties, so he and Liz kept their distance, and no one suspected anything. They figured her sister's wedding had thrown Liz for a loop, making her rethink her life choices the way major life events often do. She'd likely quit to find another job where she might have a better chance of meeting a man.

Whatever her reasons for quitting and then returning, they were relieved to have her back.

All except for Priscilla, who eyed her with a cold glance, swung her head to the side, and lifted her shoulders in a puzzling gesture. A little while later, Liz saw her with Matthew, standing much too close as she giggled and spread her hands to elaborate on the point she was describing. Matthew smiled and talked to her in a friendly way. Liz felt a pang of pity for Priscilla. Clearly, she was insecure. It wasn't unusual for the girls to be eager for Matthew's attention, but it was the first time Liz had felt animosity from one of the other workers. Did Priscilla sense that there was something between her and Matthew?

Christmas was in the air, with the whole market bustling. Cash registers whirred, and at the end of the day, Matthew was grinning at the bulging zippered bank bag.

He asked to take Liz out that Saturday evening. She said yes. He told her there would be no surprises, merely a visit to Esther's sister Verna and her husband. Over on Lampeter Road. He would pick her up in his buggy.

Mam was thrilled to have her be picked up in a buggy, with Matthew Zook no less. She offered to iron her covering, while Liz hurried upstairs for a shower. Liz riffled through the array of colorful dresses hanging in her closet before settling on a deep purple one. She slipped into it, surveyed the results, and promptly shed the imposing garment for one of a deep sea green color, fairly new and much nicer. She didn't have much time to do her hair, so she combed, rolled along the sides, gave a quick spritz of hairspray, and twisted it into a bun on the back of her head. She donned her white head covering, tied the black apron about her waist, and pulled on her thin black stockings and her shoes before she ran down the stairs, her purse and coat flying along.

"Why the hurry?" her mother asked.

"He said seven."

"Oh, well. It's almost that."

"Yes. Mam, did the little girls get into my bottles of perfume?"

"I doubt it."

"Someone did. I can't find the one I was looking for."

"I'll ask them."

"Where are they?"

"At Barbie's house for the night."

Mam watched as Liz drew the sleeves of her coat up over her arms, then buttoned it down the front, before throwing her purse strap over her shoulder. Liz could tell her mam was pleased, and that she desperately wanted the relationship to work out. Liz wanted to pause and remind her that it was just a date and that she shouldn't start planning another wedding in her mind. It would be enough to handle her own disappointment and another failed relationship without having to worry about her mam's crushed hopes and dreams for her. But Liz reminded herself that it was all in God's hands. She couldn't predict the future, nor could she control her dear mam's feelings. She would just have to trust God. Besides, Matthew's team was pulling up the driveway and she didn't want to keep him waiting.

Matthew helped Liz into the buggy, then tucked a warm blanket around her legs, keeping his arm across her lap for a moment longer than was necessary. She smiled in the darkened interior of the buggy, felt warm and giddy with nerves, as if she was sixteen again. The air was cold, but the stars twinkled in happy formations above them and the moon sailed across the sky in all its full glory as the darkened fields spread around them. White silhouettes of farms dotted the moon-washed landscape.

The horse was rather small, she thought, or the buggy was higher than normal. But what he lacked in size, he certainly made up in spirit and power, his feet hitting the macadam with a quick rhythm, his ears pointed forward as he held his head high. On either side, the headlights created white light, revealing the road, the gleaming black harness studded with silver spots, the length of the horse's back and the arching neck with the neatly combed black mane flapping gaily as he ran.

Liz loved a long buggy ride, the steady sound of hooves, the rasping rhythm of steel rims on macadam, and it was made all the lovelier by the intimacy and coziness of sharing the small space with the one she loved to be with.

She felt at ease this evening, relaxed, and leaned back against the plush seat. She listened to Matthew's soft voice as he made small talk and wondered with a sort of awe about prayers of sincerity making a great difference. Gone were the devastating winds of anxiety and mistrust, the enormous task of avoiding another hurt. What relief to give this relationship over to her Lord and Savior, the One in whom she could always place her trust. His will for her life was all that mattered. She felt, again, the blossoming of a new-found faith, like a tender rosebud turned to the sun, beginning to unfold its tender petals into the beauty of a mature flower, a creation made by God alone.

Faith is a gift, she thought. An undeserved rest for the weary. *Thank you, Lord, for this place of rest after all I went through with Ray.*

* * *

The home of Esther's sister Verna was located on Route 896, between Strasburg and Georgetown, a small stone cottage with a wide front porch nestled between two tall pines, a heavy growth of yew hedges along the front. The windows were welcoming yellow rectangles of light, the neat lawn like a carpet spread around them.

They were met by her husband, a short, portly man with a straw hat at a rakish angle, a wispy beard, and two button eyes twinkling their good humor in the headlight's gleam.

"Well, imagine this, Liz finally has a date!"

"Stop it, Elvin. Be nice to me for one evening, please." But Liz was laughing as she introduced Matthew, who Elvin had never met. No one was a stranger to Elvin, and everyone was a friend.

People had talked, the way they will, when a tall, willowy beauty like Verna had "taken" Elvin Stoltzfus when he asked her, but they all agreed that if she was attracted to his sunny personality and not out to snag the most handsome popular person in the community, well, then, good for her.

They were, indeed, the odd couple, her height a good eight inches above his. But he seemed perfectly at ease, and she loved Elvin with a genuine devotion that seemed to be mirrored in him. Matthew and Liz were welcomed warmly, felt at home in the small living room decorated with Christmas greenery and cheerful candles burning everywhere.

Esther and Henry arrived a few minutes later, with Verna greeting them with the genuine happiness of a sister. Elvin grinned from the background, the darting brown eyes missing nothing.

"So this is Henry," he said.

"Yes. Henry, meet my brother-in-law, Elvin."

They shook hands as they evaluated each other.

Elvin beamed, his round cheeks like polished apples. "Well, I hope you'll be a keeper. Esther's got a whole pile of rejects. You know, those poor chaps who were given the heave-ho."

He mimicked the tossing, and Matthew burst out laughing, a deep sound of genuine mirth and enjoyment. Poor Henry's face turned a dark shade of red, but he regained his confidence as Matthew's laugh rang out.

"I just might be the one, who knows?" he said gamely.

"Good for you, Henry," Verna said, as she shook his hand warmly. "That is exactly what we need to hear. Now, give me your coats, and I'll take them to the bedroom. Baby Jason is asleep, and I hope to keep it that way. He was a mess today. Teething, I suppose."

Liz looked around the cozy little house with the glowing candles and smooth white walls, the hand-crafted furniture and tasteful décor. A deep longing welled up in her, the longing for a place of her own. She imagined kitchen cabinets to store her endless supply of Tupperware and glass dishes, tea towels and hot pads, knife sets and cookware, all gifts from friends and relatives given over the years. How deeply satisfying it would be to be a wife and homemaker. In spite of telling herself there was nothing wrong with being single, she knew this was what she truly wanted.

She watched Matthew, who had folded his tall frame into a gray, overstuffed recliner. His hair was neatly cut, clean, the dark tresses accentuating the handsome lines of his face, his white teeth flashing as he laughed again at something Elvin was saying. And she realized with a physical ache in her chest how very much she cared about him, wanted him to be by her side forever. She wanted to cook his meals, wash his clothes, and yes, be his wife, have his children. Oh, that God would permit this.

What if He didn't? What if this feeling of a true and powerful love was dashed to the ground? Well then, He'd be there for her again. It was wrong to live in fear. She would risk her whole heart again, knowing that if it was broken, God would be her healer.

There were games and snacks and conversation, the evening enjoyed by them all immensely. Liz won the first round of Monopoly after she acquired Park Place and all four of the railroads, collecting her rent in a growing pile of one hundred dollar bills. Elvin gripped both sides of his head as he landed on the very expensive Park Place with a hotel on it, rounded the corner, and collected his much-needed two hundred dollars before landing on the first railroad which took it all away again.

"No mercy, Liz, you ruthless woman!" he shouted as he mortgaged the red properties, scraped houses off Baltimore Avenue, shaking his head in disbelief.

Matthew laughed all evening, with Elvin's crazy sense of humor setting him off every time. Henry smiled, laughing lightly here and there, enjoying the game more quietly. But over dinner he joined the conversation easily, impressing them all with his thoughtful remarks and interesting ideas.

Verna served homemade pizza, a light springy crust topped with home-canned tomato sauce, fried ground beef, pepperoni, bits of ham, mozzarella cheese, green peppers, and onion. It was thick, piping hot, and simply delicious, served with homemade potato chips and grape juice mixed with ginger ale. There were cupcakes, whoopee pies, and coconut almond bars, fresh fruit salad, and a platter heaped with cut vegetables and a creamy dip.

They discussed how hard it was to make enough money to survive in Lancaster County in the modern age. Most young couples rented a home, if they had no wealthy friend or relative to help them acquire a homeowner's loan, and then a home was often unattainable, the price of real estate skyrocketing. It was probably the main reason young couples moved to adjacent counties to buy cheaper land with less taxes, although they found wages to be lower as well. But the peace and quiet of a more sparsely settled region was often taken into consideration, the thought of raising a family in an area affording more privacy a huge factor as they came to a decision.

"Money is the root of all evil," Esther said, pouting a little.

"No, sister, you have that wrong. The *love* of money is the root of all evil, not the money itself," Verna corrected her.

"All the same."

"Uh-uh. One refers to the money, the other to the heart."

"True."

"Yeah, well, we're all going into the world, I don't care what anyone says. Amish aren't real Amish anymore," Elvin said emphatically.

"You old grouch," his wife said, surprised by his sharp observation.

"I mean it. My dad says he remembers his father and his uncles sitting around discussing trade. They were all farmers, every one. And they were arguing whether the Amish would ever be allowed to have their own stores. They said 'Never. Absolutely not.'"

Matthew looked on, his mouth compressed.

"'That'll never happen,' they said. "Look at us. Two generations down the road. We own regular Wal-Marts here in Lancaster County."

"Oh, don't be such a doomsayer," Esther told him. "We all have to make a living somehow."

"That's why we need to go west. The great wild and woolly West."

"And how are you going to make a living out there?" Verna asked.

"Turn the prairie over with my trusty steeds. Onward ho! The pioneer spirit," he answered.

"You plain down turn me off," Verna said, but her eyes twinkled.

By that time, everyone was laughing, imagining the well-fed Elvin walking behind a plow on the unforgiving prairie.

Henry joined in, and everyone listened. "But none of it is really our fault. If we're here on earth, we have to do what we can to make a living, to provide for our families, in any way we can. There wouldn't be enough land to support us all, if every Amish family owned a farm."

"That's true."

And so one discussion melded into another, until the clock showed almost two o'clock. After cups of coffee, the girls helped Verna clean up while the men went to the barn for the horses. They promised to come again soon as they waved goodbye, then climbed into buggies and headed out in opposite directions.

Liz felt closer to Matthew than she ever had. She tried not to snuggle against him, but she did lean in ever so slightly. She loved being in this buggy with him, loved the coziness of the warm space.

"Did you have fun?" he asked.

"Yes, I really did."

"That Elvin. Seriously, he is so funny. He talks an awful lot, but everything that came out of his mouth made me laugh."

"No one could understand it when Verna married him, but if you're with them, you can see why. He would be a hoot to live with."

Matthew laughed again, then quieted. "It's late, but I don't really feel like saying goodbye yet. I won't see you till after church tomorrow."

"I have church, too."

"I know. I guess the proper thing for me to do would be to drop you off and leave. It's way late."

"Probably, yes."

Suddenly he spoke seriously. "Do you believe in distant courtship?"

"I . . ." She faltered, not sure how to respond. "Do you?"

"No. But if you do, I promise to uphold your high standards."

She hesitated, then said, "Ray and I never touched. His parents were very clear on the matter. But I often wonder if that contributed to his disinterest, after dating all those years."

"I don't think it makes much difference, one way or another. I just don't think it was meant to be, you know?"

"It's not really clear in the Bible. I think it's a matter of individual conscience. Like, it's different for every couple." She didn't want to imagine him kissing his previous girlfriend, but she couldn't help it. Unconsciously, she leaned into him a bit more, feeling his sturdy warmth against her own body. He was like a magnet, pulling her to him. Never before had she felt attraction in such a physical way. In that moment, distant courtship seemed almost ludicrous. Besides, hadn't they crossed that line already, that night at the cabin when she sat in the same chair with him and leaned against him under the stars? Had that been wrong?

"How do you feel about your past relationship now, Liz?"

She picked nervously at the soft lap robe, before turning to find him searching her face.

"I don't know. I mean, sometimes I forget the pain, other times I'm sure I'll relive the exact same thing this time around."

"Does praying help?"

"A lot, actually."

"Same here."

"But when I'm with you, all the rules sort of . . . don't matter." She had spoken honestly and now felt a bit shocked by it.

"Why? Am I a bad influence?"

"No, not in that way. I just . . ."

She waved a hand. "Forget it, okay?"

"I'm not going to forget it. What do you mean?"

"I should not have said that."

He turned his horse into the driveway and sat quietly as the buggy wheels crunched on gravel, the horse's hooves tossing bits of it against the mud splasher. She shivered as the cold, white moon shone in through the window on the left of her. They rode up to the sidewalk in silence, the air drenched with the suffocating bubbles of insecurity, of what was considered proper and what was not. Liz had been dangerously close to telling him how much she wanted him, how when she was near him, all rules of what was right and what was wrong flew right out the window.

When the horse was drawn to a stop, he turned to her. "Thank you for being my date tonight. I hope there are many more to come. I enjoyed it very much."

"Thank you, Matthew. I enjoyed it, too." She drew the door back by its handle, lifted the lap robe, and slid out gracefully.

"Goodnight, Liz."

"Goodnight, Matthew."

She walked sedately to the front door, her shoulders slumped with the weariness of the late hour but most of all with the disappointment of the formal way they had ended the evening. They had both followed the rules, followed what was good and proper and accepted. He had not touched her, had not held her hand or slid a solid muscular arm along the back of the seat. She had not told him how much she loved him, or wanted him. She had not slid the palm of her hand along his waist and felt the fabric of his white wedding shirt. Why were they being more careful now than when they were at the cabin?

Perhaps she harbored a deep resentment toward Ray and his customs. Rules. Observations. Denials of the flesh. Whatever he'd called it. Well, once he'd broken up with her, he hadn't taken very long to grab up her best friend and kiss her for all he was worth. She'd told Liz all about it, wondering if he'd been the same with her, and Liz was far too embarrassed to tell her the truth.

She extracted the pins from her covering, removed it from her head, and laid it carefully on the dresser. She untied her bib apron, removed her dress, and

opened the drawer for her nightgown, then brushed
her teeth in the bathroom across the hallway.

She turned out the lamp and fell into bed, her
head filled with doubts and fears, agonizing thoughts
of her own inability to keep someone interested in
her. He hoped there were many more dates to come.
Mm-hm. Many more of these evenings where he'd
drop her off, say he enjoyed himself very much, then
go off to think about some other girl.

With Ray, she'd been too dumb to know better,
till her best friend told her. And here she was again,
in love with another man, and he was following
the same patterns. She must have the warmth of an
icicle in January. Maybe she was simply unattract-
ive. Matthew hadn't been like this at first. If Esther
hadn't been there as witness, she would think she'd
just imagined his boldness that night at the cabin.
She wrestled with her insecurities, the helpless feeling of being swept away in the howling gale of doubt,
caught in the painful cactus of fear, battered and broken by this thing called love.

Love shouldn't be this way. This difficult.

She tried to pray but felt her pain and misery blocking her prayers. She was taunted by the shame of his formal "thank you, I enjoyed it very much."

Suddenly she felt sure that Matthew would drag the relationship on for years, on and on and on, the way it had been for her and Ray, until he ran straight into her best friend's arms. And kissed her.

* * *

Church services were interminable. She heard very little of the sermon. dozed off, and almost fell off the bench, horrified to find secretive smiles and outright titters of glee moving down the row of girls. She glared at a few of the younger ones with what she hoped was a reprimand for daring to laugh at her.

After church Matthew arrived, picking her up at the sidewalk. They went to the youth's supper and singing, and afterward he brought her back to her house. She was prepared to say a formal goodbye, checking off another date in what would undoubtedly be a long row of them leading nowhere. And so she was caught off guard when he asked quietly if he could come inside.

"Oh, of course," Liz stammered.

She made coffee, hoped she could find a few cookies or bars in the pantry. Mam, however, had made provisions, just in case. She noticed Liz had prepared nothing and so took matters into her own hands. Mam firmly believed the way to a man's heart was through his stomach and so set about making fresh pumpkin pies and seasoned pretzels with cheese dip. She left it on the countertop in full view with an index card propped against it. "These are for you and Matthew" was written with a felt-tipped pen. Liz grabbed the card and crumpled it quickly, before he could see.

"Pumpkin pie. My favorite," Matthew said.

"Good. I didn't know."

Conversation flowed fairly easily, so that Liz felt the evening was a success. Little sparks of hope flared up with each look of warmth and approval, until he said it was time to go, that he had a hard day settling trusses tomorrow, and she felt the poof of every hopeful spark.

And then, she felt a flood of bravery. It had to be done. She followed him to the door and said very softly, "You asked if I believe in distant courtship."

She startled him, she knew, by the way his eyes opened wide.

"Here is my answer."

And she stepped close, put both hands to his waist, below his vest, where the fabric of his shirt was soft and warm. She had to raise herself on her toes and turn her head slightly to the left, but she was fully capable of meeting his lips halfway and keeping them there until he could know fully of her love, her need to be with him, and find out for sure if he felt the same way. When she drew back first, he reached for her again and held her very close to his heart. She could hear the thudding of his heart beneath his vest, but above the sound of it, she heard a deep sigh of relief, and the words she would never forget.

"I think I have found my soul mate."

Chapter Seven

LOVE. OH, SWEET LOVE.

Liz smiled at the words in her mind as she hung out laundry on Monday morning. She blushed at her own boldness, then smiled a wobbly tear-filled grin at his words. She felt as if she could leap and spin and twirl, reach for the moon and the stars.

She put towels through the wringer, picked up the load of whites and stuffed them into the swirling water, then turned the wringer before lifting the towels up and down to rinse them well, the floral scent of Downy wafting through the air. She imagined herself in her own laundry room, doing her own laundry. Hers and Matthew's.

The long wheel line was filled to capacity when she finished, bed sheets and pillowcases, rugs and outerwear, the laundry room having been packed with clothes. Mam had to help Mommy King on Saturday, so she had not done the usual weekend laundry, which meant there would be a mountain of it, and which meant Mam would have this strange compulsion to thrown in all the coats, rugs, and bedding she could find.

She rinsed out the washing machine, then the rinse tubs, before lowering herself to her knees to wipe up the spills and excess water.

She was starving.

Mam was at the kitchen table, drinking coffee and nipping at the shoofly pie with a spoon. Sure enough, a foil-wrapped breakfast sandwich awaited her, and she turned the burner on beneath the coffeepot before unwrapping it.

"Mm. Cheese and bacon, plenty of egg. Thanks, Ma."

"Do you have another date?"

"Yes. I do."

"Oh, good. That's so good."

Liz smiled happily, chewed, and swallowed. "We're not getting married quite yet."

"I would hope not."

Liz watched her mother dip spoonfuls of shoofly pie into her coffee, repeat the move over and over, until she'd eaten a third of the pie.

"You need to learn how to bake, Liz. It's shameful—your age and you have no idea how to make a pumpkin pie."

"Or any other pie," Liz said proudly.

"You don't even care."

"No, I don't. I dislike baking to the point where I'll do almost anything to avoid it."

"I know. But if you have a boyfriend now, you should show a bit of interest in it. You have never baked a loaf of bread, either."

"And I probably never will. Cooking is my thing, Mam. I'm good at it, and Matthew knows that. After all, he pays me good money to keep the grill going at the market."

"But every husband needs warm homemade bread," her mother protested.

"He can get it at work. We buy delicious homemade bread for our customers every day from Mark Sie Sarah."

Her mother shook her head, her lips compressed in disapproval. "Well, it's scary the way this young generation refuses to keep the old way alive, feeding their children bought white bread, buying baked goods at the market. My mother remembers grinding her own flour. Nothing was thrown away. Not a crust of bread or a teaspoon of butter."

Liz lifted the lid of her breakfast sandwich to add a slice of tomato and a dollop of mayonnaise. She poured a cup of coffee, added creamer, and sat down to enjoy her morning with her mother.

"Now, Mam, you should try and enjoy the traditions we do keep. All the church services, weddings, and funerals are exactly the way they always were. So is our dress, our way of transportation, our schools and family structure."

"Our way of dress isn't the same."

But the morning was filled with Liz's happiness, her inner confidence. She couldn't hold it in anymore, so she told her mother everything, who turned bright red and became flustered, sputtering and going to the sink to throw out her cold coffee.

"Now, you just listen here, young lady. That good Christian courtship you and Ray had was not the reason he told you off. That's just an excuse."

"Alright, Mam. You think what you want about Ray, but you aren't the one who dated him. Did you kiss Dat before you were married?"

"I don't have to answer that question."

"Uh-huh. You did."

"Well, but back then, that was how things were done."

"So I'm keeping a tradition alive."

"Oh you."

Liz laughed, then spied Sylvia making a grumpy appearance, wearing an old bathrobe, her hair loosening from the ponytail holder she'd wound around it. She was so young and so unspoiled, Liz thought. And genuinely sweet like their father. She hoped she would be spared the worst of break-ups and the many pitfalls of *rumschpringa*.

"How was your weekend, Sunshine?"

Sylvia glared at her, went to the refrigerator, and poured herself a glass of orange juice. "Good."

"What were you doing?"

"Stuff."

Liz burst into a happy laugh, and Mam couldn't help herself from joining in. Sylvia twisted a few strands of hair around and around her forefinger, sipped her orange juice, and didn't say anything.

"So what are we doing today?" Liz asked.

"Well, I thought we'd finish up the Christmas shopping. I have most everything, but there are a few things I need yet. I thought maybe we could go to Wal-Mart, maybe Country Housewares, then stop in to see Mommy. She's not doing well of late. We could take her some butter pecan ice cream. Her favorite."

Sylvia sprang to life at the thought of Christmas shopping. "Let's go to Rockvale Square. All the outlets. I need a new pair of sneakers for volleyball. Rachel has white ones. Mam, why can't I have white ones? Huh? Maria says her mom is buying her a pair."

Mam pondered this sentence before inserting the shoofly into its Ziploc bag and closing it firmly.

"I can't see Dan Sie Becca buying her daughter white shoes. You know they're against our *ordnung*, and Becca would never."

"She wears blue Crocs in the garden, so what's wrong with white sneakers?" Sylvia asked, the whine beginning in her voice.

"No, Sylvia. If I give in, it'll just be something different next week. We'll find you a pair of black ones."

Sylvia pouted prettily, went to the pantry, and returned with a box of Wheaties, poured it into a bowl, and went to the refrigerator for milk. She set aside pitchers of tea and juice, then said there was no milk.

"There's a whole tankful in the milkhouse," Liz sang out.

"You go," Sylvia said.

"Alright. Give me the pitcher."

That was what love did, she decided. It turned you into a much better person, filled up your heart with happiness that spilled over and splashed onto your friends and family. It was a blessing from God who had answered her prayers, even if she had to help Him out a bit.

* * *

Christmas was in the air. Christmas music poured out of the walls and ceilings of stores, except, of course, the Amish stores that were filled with mostly Amish women visiting, meeting old acquaintances or friends and relatives out buying *Grischdaug* (Christmas) presents.

Liz bought material for a new dress at Belmont Fabric, a brilliant color of red that made Mam frown and Sylvia jump up and down with glee, begging Liz to buy her some too. She imagined Matthew complimenting her and bought an extra three yards for Sylvia.

They bought the ice cream and arrived at Mommy's door with enough time to spare so they could put on the coffee pot and enjoy a dish with her. Mommy (grandmother) was small and bent, so frail and weak, but her blue eyes shone brightly as she received them with a soft hug, her cheek papery against Liz's, the smell of talcum powder bringing quick tears.

"Mommy, I miss you. We have to come see you more."

"Oh no. I'm never lonely. I'm not alone if the Lord is here with me. I work on my embroidery, and I get my own meals." Her eyes twinkled. "Fish and Brussels sprouts."

The girls laughed, knowing Mommy was joking. She had always enjoyed rich foods and sweets and in recent years had taken to eating frozen packaged meals from the grocery store. No one could blame her. She had spent decades cooking for her large family, always making everything from scratch. There was no harm in relaxing a bit now that she lived alone, especially with her arthritis making it hard to stand over the stove or at the sink for long periods.

"The fish are steamed, at that. With a little Old Bay," she said softly, then commenced shaking up and down with laughter again.

"Mommy, you're just a mess," Sylvia said, real admiration shining from her eyes.

"Well, even if you grow old and wrinkled and homely looking, you can still have your spirit. I have always enjoyed a good joke, always kept my sense of humor." She lifted a misshapen, arthritic finger. "Now you know the Bible says laughter is good for the soul, but a sour countenance withereth the bones. Or something close to those words. And it's true. We need to stay happy and cheerful. There is plenty of sorrow on this earth, and that is all right and good, but so is good humor."

As usual, Liz loved to listen to her grandmother, a feisty woman who had raised a family of ten children, lived through the Great Depression as a young girl, wearing dresses made of chicken-feed sacks, carrying a tin bucket to school containing buttered bread and canned peaches. Times were hard, in fact, much harder than Liz or Sylvia could imagine, but through it all, the family stayed on the farm and thrived, grew up and married, carrying the resilient spirit on to the next generation. Sometimes her grandmother would name the items invented since her birth—ordinary, everyday objects like ballpoint pens, battery-powered things, weed-eaters, plastic and the great volume of objects that brought.

Her views on religion and spirituality were quite liberal, however. She disliked the idea of any denomination being better than the other, including the Amish. Self-righteousness comes in many forms, she would remind them, wagging the crooked forefinger, and it is one of the things Jesus was very displeased with. Her view of spirituality sometimes raised a few conservative eyebrows, but everyone loved her, and everyone who came to visit went away with a smile on their face.

Not all of Mam's siblings had stayed with the Amish; some chose to pursue a church outside the Amish community, which had been hard for Mommy to accept at first, but not for very long. Mommy loved her children unconditionally and knew each was following the path he or she felt led by God to go down. So she chose to be ok with their life choices, which sometimes raised eyebrows among the more conservative folks.

"Mommy, what can we get you for Christmas this year?" Liz asked.

"I don't need anything. Please don't spend your money on me. I'll soon be gone, and then you'll have all my junk to divide."

Mam spoke up. "We are already putting our money together to get you a new recliner. You need it, badly."

"No, no. The one I have is perfectly fine."

Mam smiled at Liz, who gave her a knowing look.

The ice cream was delicious, the small house fragrant with the smell of freshly brewed coffee. Mommy brought cups and plates of cheese and crackers, chocolate cut-out cookies, and tangerines. Her collection of musical snow globes were set on the table along the wall, along with a few red candles with plastic holly and berries in a ring around them. Her tattered Bible lay on top of the yellow composition book, a basket containing cards and envelopes and stamps beside it. The table was quite cluttered with items she used, so no one was allowed to touch any of it. This was Mommy's domain, and she was ruler over her kitchen table.

Sylvia wound up every musical snow globe, resulting in unharmonious clatter as one tune ran into the next one. Mommy grinned mischievously and said, "Now, Sylvie, soon we'll have rock 'n' roll here."

They all laughed, especially Sylvia. She loved her grandmother with her whole heart and was always the first one to volunteer to help her with housecleaning or yard work.

They talked of everyday goings-on in the community. Babies born, accidents, who was hospitalized, who had begun dating, the weddings of the past November and December still to come.

"Well, I, for one, am extremely relieved to have Marianne's wedding over and done with," said Mam. "I'm no longer as young as I was, believe me. It seemed as if I had an awful time keeping my thoughts together."

"I always said doing a wedding is three-fourths headwork, and no one can do it but the mother. *Gel* (Right), Sadie?"

They exchanged a knowing look.

"Well, Liz, perhaps it will be your turn next year?" Mommy asked. "Now that you're dating, and at your age . . ."

"Don't even think about it, Mam," Liz's mother said, genuine exhaustion passing over her face.

"Of course not," said Liz decidedly. "Matthew is independent, very busy with the restaurant at market and his contractor work. Plus, we have to give it a while, make sure it's right this time."

An uncomfortable silence fell over the coziness of their grandmother's kitchen table. Liz looked up to find three pairs of eyes watching her with sympathetic expressions.

"But you do like him?" Mommy inquired kindly.

Liz nodded, her lower lip caught in her teeth, displaying her anxiety. Like? Did she like him? She loved him beyond all reason, loved him even more than she had ever loved Ray. Her emotions rode the roaring rapids of a dangerous river, her inflatable craft bouncing off the rocks of doubt into quiet pools of prayer and faith, where God's presence was so real she could almost reach out and touch Him, only to be hurled into the maelstrom of fear by the sight of Matthew, that handsome face, the aloof demeanor, the independent spirit that caused a war within her.

Yes. She liked him.

"She's gone, Mommy," Sylvia said, drawing up one knee and covering it with her skirt.

"Good. That is a good thing. You are no longer young, so your maturity will help to make this work. Good for you, Liz."

Mommy's feelings were so loving and so genuine, Liz felt the quick stab of tears in her eyes. She could truly rejoice with those who rejoiced and walk on earth in her old leather shoes and worn gray apron, filled with so much love it radiated from her like a heavenly scent. Liz hugged her grandmother a bit longer than was necessary, then patted her frail, bent back.

"Pray for me, Mommy. You know I will always need your prayers," she said, every line and wrinkle etched into her memory. Her glasses were round and wire-framed, one of the lenses chipped in the upper right corner. There was a large brown mole beneath one eye, but it only added to the dear familiar face.

* * *

At work, things were chaotic, with poor Annie puffing and wheezing as she struggled to keep up. Priscilla, on the other hand, seemed to always be taking bathroom breaks or just standing around. It drove Liz crazy, but it wasn't really her place to reprimand the other staff. She felt caught between her love and admiration for Matthew and the unfairness of the work and management of the restaurant. It was a bit awkward, dating her boss, but since she mostly stayed in the kitchen and he was usually occupied with duties in his office or in the dining area, no one else seemed to notice.

When Priscilla stretched her half-hour lunch break into closer to a whole hour, Matthew went in search of her and found her in the parking lot, sitting in a vehicle with the man in question. He brought her back, wasting no words, and gave her two weeks to straighten up and carry her share of the workload.

From the kitchen, Annie and Liz heard, "Well, I'm quitting. No boss should ever intrude on the privacy of their employee."

Annie's eyebrows raised before she snorted loud enough for both Matthew and the disgruntled Priscilla to hear. The lunch rush had died down, but there were still a few tables with guests in the dining room.

"Let's talk in my office," Matthew said, keeping his voice calm.

"There's nothing to talk about. I quit."

"I told you I'll give you another chance."

"I don't want another chance," she spat. "I'm leaving this place. There is a whole world of jobs out there for me, with better people than you Amish."

"It's your choice, Priscilla. But don't do anything you'll regret. Think of your parents, your sisters and brothers. They love you and would feel awful to see you make wrong choices."

"Ha!" Priscilla laughed bitterly. "Believe me, they don't care. My father hates me."

"No, no."

This was all overheard in the restaurant kitchen behind the double swinging doors. Annie's eyes opened wide. Liz tried to stay focused on chopping cucumbers for salads, lifting a silent prayer for Matthew to speak and act with wisdom. Then Matthew's voice fell and Liz and Annie couldn't make out the words. But shortly after, Priscilla pushed open the kitchen doors and announced bitterly, "I'm done here. I'll be back for the van ride home." And with that, she grabbed her coat off the rack and left.

Priscilla did return in time for market van, sitting in a corner of the very back seat. She shut out the world with earplugs and kept entirely to herself. As Priscilla exited the van at her home, Liz said goodbye, that it had been nice working with her, but received no response except a hard slam of the door.

After Priscilla left, Matthew hired a young woman named Miriam, shy and very pretty. Her blond hair appeared bleached, her blues eyes like jewelry, shining and gleaming with the kaleidoscope of emotions she kept in check. A proficient worker, Liz soon sensed Matthew's admiration, and she could not keep the jealousy from creeping into her heart. She noticed every time Matthew spoke to Miriam, which seemed to be far more often than necessary. Certainly far more frequently than Matthew spoke to Liz at work.

She was not her usual self on Saturday evening, so when Matthew inquired about her well-being, she told him she was not feeling well, coming down with something likely. She did not go to church but lay in her room with a box of tissues and no faith to think of the future, her peace and confidence shattered by Matthew's admiration of Miriam. The more she thought about it, the more convinced she became that he was falling in love with Miriam.

She went downstairs to escape the worst of her misery, made a cup of spearmint tea, and scalded her tongue. She stood at the kitchen window and stared across the bleak brown lawn, planning how she would confront Matthew about his feelings for Miriam as she watched two squirrels chase each other up and down the trunk of a tree.

She knew her thoughts were bitter when she thought humans were no better than squirrels, chasing each other around and around. The only difference was human beings had feelings, and human beings created a world of hurt for others so much of the time. Thoughtless. Matthew was thoughtless, the way he strung Liz along while clearly falling for another girl. Just like Ray. Well, she was no longer the gullible person she had been the first time around. The ball was in her court this time, and she would not get hurt. She stopped crying, squared her shoulders, and solidified her resolve.

She would be courageous. She would allow Matthew to find real love. Wasn't that the noble thing to do? "If you love someone, let them go." She'd read that somewhere a long time ago.

Esther had left a message for her on her parents' voicemail, so Liz dutifully donned her heavy sweater, a pair of boots that were a few sizes too big, and galumphed across the lawn to the office where her father did his bookwork and kept his guns and archery equipment, as well as his books and catalogues. This was where the telephone was housed, since it was forbidden by the *ordnung* of the church to keep one in the house.

"Hey, Esther."

"What's up, Liz?"

"Not much."

"Well, it looks as if we have acquired real boyfriends, and Christmas is only a few weeks away. Boyfriends require Christmas gifts. So, what do you think about shopping on Wednesday evening? Want to?"

A long pause.

"Are you there?"

"Yes."

"Why don't you answer me?"

"Well, I don't . . . I don't know. It doesn't suit me Wednesday. I have plans."

"No, you don't. What's wrong?"

"Nothing."

"Why can't you go?"

"Because I don't want to. I don't need a gift. By Sunday evening I'm not going to . . . have . . ."

Here the line remained silent, with Esther holding the receiver away from her ear, shaking it, then yelling, "Are you there?" When no sound came through, she felt like Alexander Graham Bell, yelling through the new invention. "Good grief, Liz. Are you there?"

"I'm here."

A sorry little voice, nose stuffed up. She was crying. Liz was actually sobbing now, hiccupping pitifully, like a child.

"I'm coming. I'm coming over now, Liz. I don't know what's going on, but clearly the phone isn't going to cut it."

* * *

Liz was in her room, curled up on the small sofa against the north wall, an afghan around her shoulders and a fleece throw across her lap, her legs tucked up, the picture of abject misery. Her nose was swollen and red as an apple, her eyes rimmed in the same color, puffy and irritated by frequent dabs of crumpled Kleenex.

"Liz. What's going on?"

Esther bent down for a warm hug, then sat close beside her as fresh tears coursed down Liz's cheeks, the kindness releasing a new wave of emotion. Esther allowed Liz time to compose herself before shivering, then going to the windows to see if they were locked. A cold draft of air was coming through to both of them, so she pushed down on the windows, turned the locks, and sat down again.

"Esther, I'm . . ."

Liz drew a steadying breath, then poured out the story of the attractive Miriam and Matthew's admiration of her, how she had to stay ahead of the curve by telling him the friendship was over.

"I can't take another heartbreak. And it's bound to happen. He already avoids me at market. He talks about her all the time."

"But have you prayed?"

"I try. But I'm so afraid. I can't find any faith at all. I'm completely awash in negative thoughts." She held up a hand to silence Esther, as she opened her mouth to speak. "No. Don't reassure me. Just don't."

"Alright. I understand. You've been hurt badly, and what's that old saying? 'Once bitten, twice shy,' or something like that."

"That's exactly how it is."

"But you're jumping to conclusions, Liz. You are."

"Have you ever seen Miriam? Do you know her?"

"I know her parents. She goes with the Eagles."

"I don't care which group she belongs to, Matthew will follow her anywhere."

"But he doesn't want her, Liz."

"You don't know that, and neither do I. Why would I go out and buy him a Christmas gift to have him come white-faced and embarrassed, returning the whole lot after he gets up the nerve to tell me he's done with me, it's not working out, he's 'sorry.'" She made air quotes with her fingers.

Esther kicked off her shoes, drew her knees up, and rested her hands on them. She shivered again. "Your room is freezing."

Without answering, Liz handed her another fleece throw, grabbed another handful of Kleenex, and snorted harder than necessary. Esther slanted her a look.

"Well, if you're so bound and determined he is in love with Miriam, then I suppose it wouldn't be smart to go out and buy a gift. But I am not convinced, Liz. I think it's all your imagination."

"But why would he avoid me? He does it all day long," Liz wailed, caught up in a fresh wave of dashed hopes.

"Maybe he thinks it isn't proper to be seen together there, now that you're dating. The other staff don't even know you two are together, do they?"

"I think you're wrong. I think he is falling for Miriam, hard, and he's too much of a coward to tell me."

"Really?"

"Really."

Esther was quiet, almost persuaded by the assurance in Liz's voice. They sat together, side by side, sharing the feeling of insecurity, of loss. Esther really had no idea whether or not Liz was right, so there wasn't much to say.

Finally, Esther noticed the absence of the wall clock with the ornate woodworking. "Hey, whatever happened to the clock Ray gave you?"

"I made him take it back. The ticking drove me nuts."

Esther nodded. "I won't settle for less than a grandfather's clock."

A clock is the Amish version of an engagement ring, but in that moment Esther and Liz were both painfully aware of their own clocks ticking, the time slipping away, their futures uncertain.

Chapter Eight

THE NEXT MORNING AT MARKET WAS ROUGH, seeing Matthew's handsome face, the flashing smile and warm light in his eyes as he greeted her. His smile slid away after she mumbled an unintelligible reply.

She shivered as she turned the lights on, then bent to turn on the grill and the oven. Annie pushed open the swinging doors, deposited her purse and sweater on her side of the shelf by the row of hooks. She rubbed her hands together, then headed for the coffee maker without as much as a single word. Liz didn't let that bother her at all, there would be plenty of words once she got started, but she wondered how she could possibly get through the day watching Matthew and Miriam. Their names even matched. She felt a fresh wave of despair.

Dear God in Heaven, give me courage. Give me strength. A thousand times she had begged God, but it seemed her prayers always ascended to the ceiling and then fell at her feet. Why? Why was she left empty?

But she carried on, making the home fries, frying sausage patties to a golden brown, one ear open to Annie's speculations as she stood stirring the large pot of chipped beef gravy.

Annie was having serious hip problems, tilting from side to side like a floundering craft in swollen water. She seemed quiet, without the usual appetite and bluster, no interesting tidbit to relay from other women looking in on the goings-on of the community. It wasn't gossip, she assured her. She would never gossip. Why, the Bible clearly told us that gossip was evil. Her mouth took on the self-righteous tilt it normally did when she touted the *Schrift* (scriptures), and she felt justified, felt herself a very good Christian indeed.

And she was, really. Except for the lively interest she had in others' goings on. She was close to many people, a friend to all, filled with the confidences of trusting, troubled women, but she couldn't keep this tantalizing information to herself. She would always end a new bit of information with, "So you can help me pray for Anna [or Ruth or Sarah or whoever had poured out her heart to her]," and so it felt to her more like bearing one another's burdens than gossip.

Annie popped a slice of whole wheat toast out of the toaster, then spread a liberal amount of butter and upended the plastic honey bear.

"I don't want a hip replacement, but the way this is going, I'll have to see an orthopedic surgeon soon. I can't live with this pain, and all that Advil isn't good either. Rueben sie Mary told me she would take that new thing, I can't think of the name, you know how it's always the next new herbal thing. They don't work." She paused to stuff the last of the toast into her mouth, before rolling her eyes. "If you ask me, she needs to add some sugar to those children's diets. White-faced and skinny, living on that stuff they do. Only saying. But you know, Liz, I went Christmas shopping with Mary, our Mary, the one who never has any money. I gave her a couple of hundred dollars." Here she paused to purse her lips with her own goodness, waiting for the response that was sure to come.

"Why, Annie, that was very generous of you."

"Oh, now, Liz. Any mother would do that. But as I was saying, walking through all those stores, my hip was on fire, or felt like it. I told Mary I had to sit down, so we ate at Wendy's. I love their burgers. The one with two hamburgers on it. With cheese. They have awful good coffee. Mary got a salad. Can you imagine going to Wendy's and getting a salad? That is such a waste of money. She barely used any dressing, the only thing that makes a salad edible."

By this time, Liz had stopped listening almost completely, could not have repeated a word Annie said, but she kept nodding and smiling, inserting an occasional, "Really?"

Out of the corner of her eye, she watched Miriam in a pale pink dress and white apron, a vision of loveliness with her blond hair and blue eyes as she spoke to Matthew, pointing to the farthest table. She saw him nod, before they both vanished from sight. She bent to turn on the steam tables.

"Boy, Liz, that Miriam looks like an angel. Or what I imagine they look like."

Thanks. Thanks a lot, Liz thought, but went back to the grill without answering.

The day was too long and much too hard, so that she felt exhausted by evening and fell into the van with relief. She could view the back of Matthew's head as he sat quietly without conversing with the driver.

So this was her last ride home from market. Tonight, she would end the friendship, allow him the space to follow his heart. Matthew and Miriam. The perfect couple. If it was God's will that she remain single, then she would bow her head and say, "Thy will be done." Yes, she could do that with the help of the Lord. It was a small sacrifice compared to the ultimate sacrifice of Jesus giving His life, crucified in a cruel way to release the bonds of sin. She could give her life for Him, serve Him as she carried her own cross.

It would be a relief, to be rid of the doubts and fears, the constant struggling to avoid the feeling of being let down, the raw emotion so taxing on her well-being. Single girls lived a life of total freedom, so there was that to look forward to.

She would no longer be able to work at the restaurant, not with Miriam there. No doubt, Matthew would begin his friendship with her at the earliest opportunity, although not without waiting the proper time. She could feel the sense of desolation beginning to creep over her but knew this time she would be strong, accustomed to the ways of the broken heart.

* * *

When he arrived a few minutes past seven, she went out to greet him in the usual manner, made small talk as she helped him unhitch, then led the way to the house, where her parents greeted him warmly. The little girls were shy, staying in the background, Matthew an object of awe. He was a boyfriend, so he was extra special.

They went upstairs to her room, to sit on the sofa provided for the purpose of having friends over. This was not unusual in the Amish culture, to have young men upstairs in a girl's room, although it varied among families, same as many other things. Liz was glad for the privacy of her room, with the very serious business at hand.

She noticed Matthew's nervousness, his inability to relax, and she knew for sure. Normally, he sat back, kicked off his shoes, smiling, affable, but tonight he sat on the edge of the couch, jumped up repeatedly to find a Lifesaver in his jacket pocket, open or close a window, commenting on the cold or the wind, or any mundane thing that made no sense. Finally, when the level of unease became almost unbearable, she took a deep breath and began.

"Matthew."

He visibly jumped. "Yes?"

"I think it's time we had a serious discussion."

"Of course. Yes, I agree."

Liz cleared her throat, gave a small cough, picked nervously at the tassel of a throw pillow. "I can't see our . . ."

Quickly, he cut her off. "Liz, let me go first, okay?"

"But, I know why you're so nervous, Matthew. You don't have to hide it from me anymore."

A look of hope poured over his face, a visible brightening of his eyes. "But you don't think it's too soon? I mean, what will your parents say? I'm so worried about your mother. Mams tend to go off the deep end about things like this."

Liz waved a hand. "Don't worry, Matthew, she's been through this before. She's very spiritually minded when it comes to these things. She's strong."

"But she just had to do a wedding last month."

"A wedding? What?"

They both stopped, turned to face each other on the couch. Both began to speak at the same time, then stopped.

"You go first," Matthew said gently.

"No. You say what's on your mind. I know what it is, Matthew. I know the feelings you have for Miriam. I'm prepared to let you go, to follow your heart. It would be wrong for me to try to stop you."

"What? Miriam? What are you talking about? Why would I have feelings for Miriam?"

"Well, you do. I mean, she's so pretty and such a good worker, and you don't come back to the kitchen anymore. You avoid me at work, so I . . ."

"Liz, oh Liz. No! That's not even . . . no. Did you really think that?"

"But . . ."

"No. The reason I am here tonight is to tell you again what I told you that amazing night. When I left. What you did."

Liz felt the warmth rise in her cheeks, felt a deep humility.

"I told you I had found my soul mate."

He reached for her hand. Shocked, she allowed him to hold it.

"I love you, Liz. Miriam is a good worker, yes, but she's not my soul mate. I have no special feelings for her. Please believe me. I didn't mean to avoid you at market—I just didn't want to be too bold in front of the other staff. Liz," here he paused, looking deeply into her eyes. "I am asking you to marry me. I want you to be my wife. And I don't think we need a long engagement, given our age."

Liz was without a comprehensible thought in her head. She was so shocked, she honestly thought she might faint. And then he got down on one knee without releasing her hand, looked at her with all the love and longing of a man in love, and said very softly and gently, "Will you marry me, Liz?"

Liz could not speak at all. She opened her mouth a few times and closed it again, before two droplets like jewels appeared on her lower lashes, before dropping gently on her pale cheeks.

"Matthew, I . . . Oh my."

She gave up and allowed the tears to fall. She tried to speak but could only nod as her eyes shone into his. He drew her to her feet and placed his arms around her, kissed away the tears, murmured his love so softly, before he kissed her lips, sealing their love forever. And she laughed and cried and said, "Yes, yes, yes. I will be your wife, Matthew."

They did not say much afterward but simply gazed into each other's eyes to fully comprehend the enormity of what had occurred.

"A Christmas engagement," mused Matthew. "What could be better than the gift of your love?" Then he paused, hesitating. "Liz, I would like to be married on Valentine's Day. It's on a Thursday. I know it's soon, but . . ."

Liz nodded, understanding the mention of her mother.

"Mam will blow a fuse," she said, laughing now.

"She will. That's what I'm afraid of. She just got through a wedding last month. But I don't want to wait. Do you?"

"No, I've waited long enough," Liz laughed. "Let's talk to my mam. I bet we can convince her it's better to do it sooner than later. After all, the place is still pretty clean from my sister's wedding. If we wait a year, we'll have to start over from scratch!"

"What if your parents feel we haven't dated long enough?"

"I don't think that will be an issue," Liz answered. "Mam thinks you're wonderful."

They were grinning as they made their way down the stairs to talk to her parents, who were reading on their recliners, in that area between wakefulness and sleep, their pre-bedtime slumber, as Liz called it.

Her mother snapped awake, blinked her eyes, and hurriedly reached for the lever of the recliner, placed her feet on the floor, and stretched her housecoat across her knees, then took the palms of her hands to smooth the graying hair.

"Oh my. Excuse me. We're acting like the elderly tonight."

She started getting to her feet, but Matthew waved a hand.

"No, no, don't get up."

Her father simply opened his eyes, and a wide smile spread across his face. "What gives?" he asked.

Matthew followed Liz to the sofa, where they sat close together, watching both parents with trepidation.

"Well . . ." Matthew paused, suddenly sounding nervous. "I guess there's no way to ease into this question. What do you think of a mid-February wedding?"

"Us? You mean us?" her mother asked. When she could find no other words, she simply wagged a forefinger at Matthew, then Liz, her eyebrows raised in bewilderment.

"You and Liz?"

"It appears so," Matthew said calmly, smiling again now.

"Oh, wonderful! But wait, you can't get married. You just started dating. What will people say?"

It was always her mother's biggest concern, upholding her family's good reputation with old-fashioned pride. Everything needed to be properly done in order and according to custom, or people would talk.

"They will say a lot," Liz laughed softly. "They will speculate and surmise and suppose. They're entitled to it. But Mam, both of us are older than most marrying couples. Do you really think there's so much wrong with getting married in February?"

Dat settled it. "Why of course not. We're so ready to get you out of the house, you can have a Christmas wedding. I don't think too many spiders have taken up residence in the shop since the last wedding."

Matthew grinned, then broke into a laugh.

Mam put a hand to her chest and took a deep breath. "Elmer, we cannot have a wedding in a week and a half. It simply isn't *meeglich* (possible)."

"Why sure we could. Butcher a couple chickens. Liz has enough dresses for two dozen weddings!"

But he was teasing, and Liz reassured her parents. Their engagement was a Christmas engagement, and the wedding would be a Valentine's Day wedding.

Mam got up, bustled over to the calendar on the wall, flipped pages, counted days, and turned to face them with a panicked expression.

"Seven weeks!" she shrieked.

"No, you're wrong. Here, let me have a look," Dat said, before lumbering across the room to correct his wife's calculations.

Matthew smiled at Liz, and she smiled back, still trying to comprehend all that had occurred in the last hour. They talked with their parents awhile, before heading to the kitchen to make coffee and for the chance to engage in a private conversation about their future. Liz found herself listening as Matthew talked about his plans, still unable to really believe she had been elevated from the dutiful breakup she had set for herself to this dreamlike existence where Matthew's love surrounded her in soft billows.

"I guess I knew from the moment I saw you that there was something special about you, and it didn't take me long to figure it out. You are truly the one God has for me. I have never doubted. I believe our blessings will multiply in the years to come, with you by my side."

"Oh my," Liz sighed. "I'm only trying to take it all in. How can I think straight? I don't ever want to move forward, thank you very much. I'll just stay right here, right now, in this bubble of bliss."

* * *

It surprised Liz how unbreakable the wonderful bubble actually was. She tried very hard to keep her feet on the floor, but half the time, she found herself floating dreamily, her head and heart filled with the wonder of Matthew. And when she came home from work the following weekend, and he followed her into the house, she found an enormous grandfather's clock standing in a corner of the living room. She stood speechless, her mouth opening and closing.

"Mathew," she sighed quietly.

She felt his hand on her waist, and she turned to lean against him, gazed into his eyes, and said a heartfelt thank you.

"I'm not worth such an expensive gift," she whispered.

"Oh, but, Liz, you are worth far more than that. I can never count your worth."

Surrounded by the curious family, Liz went to the beautiful clock and plucked the card from the stream of ribbons and bows. A real card, like the one she'd received from Ray. She had to fight the feelings of dread, had to put behind her the inability to trust any card with flowery prose, declarations of a love as artificial as a plastic rose.

She opened it slowly, pretended to read the words, but found her eyes unfocused, her mind unable to comprehend. Later, alone in her room, she could read the words, trace the underlinings with a forefinger, and pray away the onslaught of doubt and low self-worth. She knew that if she was unable to battle this now, she would always be harnessed to negative thoughts, even after marriage.

And so she prayed for courage and strength.

* * *

She was unprepared for the state of panic her mother had managed to achieve, bristling with plans,

obsessed with everything this unexpected engagement required of her. She had risen from her bed
at the unusual hour of 3:30 a.m., stomped around
the house gathering clothes hampers and used towels, started up the wringer washer, and had gotten
all the laundry on the line long before the sun broke
through the wintry clouds.

She hadn't slept a wink, she said. Well, dozed,
maybe, eyeing Liz guiltily.

"I'm sorry. Mam. Really."

"Oh, no, no. Don't be. I'm so happy for you,
for all of us! It's just that Christmas is here, and I'm
not ready. I invited my side for New Year's, and I
honestly think I won't be capable. It's too much.
Well, today, first off, I have to finish my Christmas
shopping, so we may as well go to Belmont and pick
out your wedding dress, get the white capes and
aprons ordered. Sylvia will be *nāva sitza*, of course.
With whom?"

As her mother's mind spun like a frenzied windmill, Liz calmly poured a cup of coffee, added a nice
dollop of flavored creamer, and sat quietly, her eyes
shining at her mother.

"Mam, it will be fine, okay? First things first. It's a beautiful day, so we'll focus on laundry and list-making. We'll plan the whole thing in our heads. Matthew will have a list of his relatives by Friday."

"Well, we should get on the road today."

"Tomorrow. There's no use rushing ahead before we have plans."

With Sylvia's help, the little girls were combed, their black aprons pinned around their waists, and given a plate of scrambled eggs and bacon, before being bundled into their winter coats and head scarves. With dishes washed and the house straightened, they put on a fresh pot of coffee and began the wedding plans.

They made a list of relatives and appointed them to various tasks, everyone a cog in the well-oiled mechanism of an Amish wedding. Two aunts would be in charge of the enormous wooden chests containing all the wedding dishes that traveled throughout the community during wedding season. Dishes had to be counted, tables had to be set as a trial run the day before the actual wedding, replaced and recounted the day after. There were the *hossla*, the boys or young men who helped unhitch horses, stable them, and feed and water them. Who would be *die roascht leid* and *die grumbare leid* (couples to make the chicken filling and the mashed potatoes)? Who would make the celery and gravy and pepper slaw? Every job had an appointed person or group of people.

Then there was the task of ordering the vast amount of food, which Mam wanted to do that day, especially the chickens, but Liz thought it best to wait till after Christmas.

"Oh, that's right. There's still Christmas. *Hesslich* (seriously), Liz."

Mam became quite agitated, said she wasn't going to sit around all afternoon to think about this, she was going right out and calling a driver, and they were *avva* (after all) going shopping to finish up Christmas and buy all the fabric for the wedding. Whereupon, she shrugged into her coat, tied a heavy scarf around her head, jutting her chin out in order to tie it tight enough before marching off to the phone. When she returned, she told Sylvia she had to stay here to get the laundry in and help Dat with the milking, which threw Sylvia into a genuine tantrum, voicing her martyrdom in wails of denial. Mam remained firm, and Sylvia gave up, although not willingly.

As Mam went from store to store, Liz floated along on her lofty cloud of newfound happiness, not caring about too much of anything, including the fabric for her wedding dress. She would be married in sackcloth, in anything, really, but she chose a beautiful shade of deep purple, in a heavy fabric that would be very classy, indeed.

Her mother tried to be plain, but she wasn't, the way her eyes shone when she said how neatly they could press the pleats and how nice it would look with a new white *halsduch und shots* (cape and apron). Their last stop was a furniture store to buy a recliner for Matthew, something Liz would want for her own house, a thought that filled her with even more joy.

Imagine, she thought, finding Matthew in his chair, relaxed, talking about their day, her own husband to love and cherish as they grew old together. What had she done to deserve such a blessing?

She asked her mother, who eyed her levelly and said, "Nothing, of course. Everything is a gift, and we

are unworthy." Then she stopped to talk to a pass-
erby, and that was the end of that.

The very next day, Mam was cutting and sewing, going on and on about how this was just highly
unusual. Every wedding she had ever done, or known
of, the sewing was done by July or August, and the
wedding was not until November.

Hesslich, she repeated at frenzied moments.
Hesslich.

Liz grinned dreamily, apologized for the incon-
venience, but didn't much care. She was marrying
Matthew, and that was all that mattered. She knew
deep down her mother was thrilled, loved the attention, the surprise, and ongoing congratulations, the
women who shook her hand and said, "Surely you'll
manage."

The grandfather's clock chimed deeply, a bell-
like quality that struck chords of joy in Liz's heart.
It stood in a corner of her room, a testimony to the
fact that disappointment and sorrow could be overcome, replaced by a deep gratefulness and realization
of every blessing. She wrapped the recliner in gold
ribbon and attached silver bows and sprigs of holly

berry. She wrote of her love in a gorgeous card, then led Matthew to the living room on Christmas Eve. He sat in it, then reached up to pull her onto his lap, as her family looked on, smiling and laughing, clapping at her discomfiture. He loved the chair, he said, then took her aside to tell her he loved her much more than the chair.

Was there ever a Christmas Eve such as this?

A soft sprinkling of snowflakes had begun in the late afternoon, the world hushed, muffled by the sound of the drifting snow, the atmosphere never quite dark the way night should be. Cars drove slowly, horses' hooves sounded muted, a dull *thock thock* in the falling snow.

Matthew and Liz walked to the pond, through the harvested cornfields now dressed in a heavy green crop of rye. It was a white, magical world, the steadily falling snow turning the landscape into a winter wonderland.

Matthew hummed the song, and Liz began to sing softly. He held her gloved hand and squeezed so hard, she said, "Ow."

He stopped walking and held her against him, told her in a voice rough with emotion how much he loved her and how he did not deserve so much happiness. They were both in awe of this night, of God and the great love He had for His children.

"It's hard to believe, Matthew. How God is so faithful. No matter how dreary and hopeless our lives can be. He always rewards us in one way or another."

"My darling Liz, you are the greatest gift I have ever received for Christmas. I just hope I can be worthy of you in the days to come."

And Liz could not answer, knowing the tears would come first.

Chapter Nine

THE CHRISTMAS ENGAGEMENT WAS ANNOUNCED in church in the end of January. The deacon spoke in the usual tradition, how two believers had agreed to step into holy matrimony, where the wedding would be held, and when. Then her father spoke up, his rumbling voice deep with emotion, inviting all those sixteen years and older, inviting the beloved close community to their daughter's wedding.

The church service was concluded with the last song, which seemed to reverberate through the shop with special fervor. Everyone was so happy for Elmer and Sadie's Liz, the poor thing having been jilted so cruelly. And such a nice girl.

Matthew and Liz did not attend church services the day they were *aus groofa* (announced), as tradition dictated. But the family all came home for a special celebratory supper that evening, as they all rejoiced and were in high spirits at the thought of the upcoming wedding.

Samuel fussed worse than an old lady, Sylvia told him, the way he carried on about *nāva-sitzing* with Matthew's sister.

"She's too old," he wailed. "And she's tall enough that she could probably carry me in."

He did not laugh when everyone else did.

"I mean it, you guys. I'm short. It's gonna look so odd."

Matthew wiped his yes. "She's not much taller than you are, Sam. Plus, you might grow an inch or so yet."

"Can't you let someone else do it. I could help the *hossla*."

"Not really, Samuel."

Liz took pity on her brother, although she really did want him to be *nāva sitza*. She looked at Matthew, who looked back at her and suddenly raised his eyebrows.

"I don't know," he mused. "I could ask my best friend, Henry."

Liz nodded. "He's dating Esther, but for one day, would it matter?"

"I know Rachel wouldn't mind," Matthew added.

When Samuel got the slightest whiff of being let off the hook, he whooped and yelled so loudly, Dat had to calm him down with a stern look and a few words of reproach.

Liz cleaned the house from top to bottom, Sylvia in tow, who displayed an alarming amount of reluctance and rebellion for one old enough to be taught the ways of an Amish wedding. She balked at washing the upstairs windows, saying they just washed them in November when Marianne got married, and it had hardly rained since.

"You know how near I fell out of these windows in November?" she asked, her fists propped on her hips as she glared at Liz.

"I'll do it. Here, you dust. Be sure and move everything."

And so it went.

The yard was raked and the garden edged to perfection, limp brown tillage radishes bringing a promise of loose, loamy soil in spring. The snows of January had melted into an unusually spring-like week in February, which brought a great amount of outside work, putting Mam into a finely turned dither.

"What a slop. Seriously, if this warm weather keeps up, we are going to have an extremely muddy wedding. That back field where the buggies will be parked will be nothing but a sea of mud. Even a few horses and *hossla* will churn up that old dead grass. Samuel doesn't have a decent pair of boots. Oh, Liz. Did you know Elam sie Anna had a miscarriage? She's not going to be able to make the tapioca. Now what? Ruthie does a better job anyways. Should I ask her? What do you think, Liz?"

Liz looked at Sylvia, who took Mam's hand and led her to the recliner. "Sit down, Mam, before you start crying. You're tired. Liz will call Ruthie. Anna can't help it that she miscarried. Poor thing. I'm sure she needs some time."

Mam wept a few tears of exhaustion and fell into a deep sleep, her mouth hanging open as snores of mammoth proportion sounded through the house, much to the girls' relief.

Matthew lived there at the farm with Liz and her family from the time the wedding was announced at church services until the day they would move to their own home. This, too, was an old tradition, the groom readily available to help with the work preparing for the wedding and any harvesting still to be done. Of course, with the wedding in February, there was no harvesting, so he went to work with Henry or to the restaurant, helping out in the evenings.

Liz loved having him there, packing his lunch, washing his clothes, and helping Mam plan the meals. It was like a preview of marriage in a way, a time of becoming acquainted to his everyday habits.

He got up out of bed very early, spent a long time brushing his teeth. He showered in the evening, not in the morning the way Samuel did. He drank copious amounts of orange juice, drank his coffee black, and ate two sweet bologna sandwiches every day, on whole wheat bread with Swiss cheese, mustard, mayonnaise, and pickles. He was ridiculously handsome in the morning, with tousled hair, his eyes slightly swollen with sleep, his teeth freshly brushed and pearl white.

He never came to her room, never kissed her, or showed any sign of affection in front of her family, but remained the perfect gentleman, which was required of him, the prospective groom. Sylvia laughed a lot when he was around, became an animated conversationalist, and tossed her head when she told Liz he was awful cute.

The few days before the wedding, the days when everyone scrambled to finish the last-minute jobs, Samuel announced unexpectedly they were calling for the biggest snowstorm of the year.

"Oh, come on," Mam pleaded, her voice rising an octave.

"No, seriously, Mam."

"Who told you?" Sylvia asked. "Your phone? You know what, Sam? You haven't had that thing long enough to know how to look for local weather. You sixteen-year-olds and your precious phones."

"Let's see it," Dat said, his eyebrows drawn down in that certain way, which meant he was the one in authority. Samuel dug around in his pocket, brought out his phone and began pressing buttons with his thumbs. Normally a cell phone was kept a discrete distance from disapproving fathers, but this was a bit of an emergency, so they all crowded around to view the forecast.

"Sure enough," Dat said.

"Ten to twelve inches!" Mam shrieked.

"Windy," Matthew said.

Liz felt her heartbeat accelerate, then settle into a loud thumping, but she said nothing. The perfect Christmas engagement, a Valentine's wedding, and now this ominous forecast.

"Horses can get through anything," Sylvia said airily.

Dat considered this. "It's true," he said suddenly.

They debated back and forth, raising concerns, discussing possible solutions. In the end, they decided to keep the wedding date, come what may.

* * *

Sure enough, the morning of before the wedding, the sky in the East was a solid wall of flaming red.

"Red in the morning, the sailor's warning," Mam said grimly, as she comforted herself with another slice of shoofly pie, sloshing hot, creamy coffee over the dish.

"We'll be alright," Matthew said. "It'll be an adventure."

Liz smiled at him, although she felt a bit shaky inside.

The door opened, and Henry appeared, laughing at the family's surprise. "You're still eating breakfast? I'm here to wash celery!"

"Sit down, Henry. Pull up a chair," Dat boomed, and Mam hurried to get him a cup of coffee, a huge square of ham and egg casserole.

"Oh good. Thank you. I'm freezing. I brought the skid loader from work, with a blade. We'll keep everything open once the snow starts. We'll just keep it going most of the day."

Mam visibly relaxed. For one wild moment, Liz thought she would actually hug Henry, she became so effusive in her voiced appreciation. Dat laughed, said that would be a job for Uncle Leroy, he loved that type of thing.

And with Henry's arrival, the rest of the relatives swarmed into the farm, armed with large kettles, roasting pans, excitement, and good humor. This was a wedding, a real wedding for Liz. She was hugged and patted and congratulated. Wedding gifts were hidden in corners until the afternoon, when the wedding gift area was completed.

Roascht leid arrived to prepare the forty plump chickens to be roasted after being stuffed with filling. A great mound of bread cubes, celery, butter, eggs, cooked livers and gizzards ground with a meat grinder, the men and women working along a lengthy table, spirits high, everyone in a good humor, making the *roascht*, the star of the wedding dinner.

Matthew and Liz, with the *nāva sitza*, tore apart the many clumps of celery, washed it well, and carried it to the aging aunts who sat at a table with sharp paring knives and cutting boards, cutting the stalks into bite-size pieces for the four heaping kettles for the creamed celery, a specialty dish reserved mostly for weddings.

Everyone had their job assigned to them, and they all went briskly about their work. Five propane gas stoves were set up in the cooking area, with plastic folding tables set up as counter space. Fussy aunts mixed pecan pie filling, while others mixed the pie crust. As if by magic, huge containers of many different varieties of cookies appeared on the shelves, cabbage, three fifty-pound bags of potatoes, stacks of butter, containers of salt, pepper, so many groceries, so much to manage.

Beside the back door to the cooking area, a generator rumbled to life, the cooler-freezer on wheels doing its job. It was a white trailer, a walk-in cooler with shelves, a large freezer for ice cream or whatever would need to be frozen. A perfect wonder, that trailer, appreciated by anyone making a wedding at home.

The men in the large shop were figuring out which seating would be best, writing down the length of tables and what size benches would be needed to turn a church service into a dining area in a matter of minutes. The entire shop was turned into a hive of worker bees, buzzing with conversation and the aura of anticipation surrounding a wedding.

Matthew and Liz smiled and laughed, beamed their happiness, but seemed a bit dazed, befuddled by the immensity of the task before them. It seemed almost impossible to actually carry off the four-hundred-guest wedding, complete with two full-course meals. Matthew grinned when Liz suggested they simply go to the Justice of the Peace and get married before the snow arrived.

"You want to?" he asked.

"Of course not," she laughed.

There was a coffee break at nine o'clock, compete with cookies and bars, a few bowls of pretzels and trays of cubed cheese, before everyone went back to work. Lunch was brought in by friends of the family, a casserole made of ground beef, shredded potatoes, and cheese. There was a green salad and bowls of potato salad. Dessert was cake, a creamy cornstarch pudding, and fruit salad.

In the afternoon, they all went to their own homes, leaving Mam to sigh with relief and dig in, setting everything right. She had her list, and kept it nearby as she organized, swept floors, cleaned the tops of tables, and provided everything anyone had forgotten.

Liz, did you find the tortillas for the wraps? Marianne, do you have enough Cool Whip for the date pudding? She scurried around, fueled by too many cups of coffee and too many peanut butter cookies, until she found nothing amiss. Dat knew there was no use trying to calm her down, it just riled her up more, so he stayed out of the way, tried to appreciate what his good *hausfrau* (housewife) did for him.

Marianne helped Liz put the finishing touches on the décor surrounding the wedding gift area, completed the white swags above the framed mirrors, helped put the candy and mints in tiered dishes.

"Are you ready for your day?" she asked, smiling at Liz.

"I sure am. I can barely wait to be Matthew's *frau*, to live in our house together."

She elbowed Liz and raised her eyebrows suggestively. "And to sleep in his bed?"

"Of course, Marianne. I'm not ashamed to admit it," she laughed.

"Did Mam give you 'The Book'? Capital THE. Capital BOOK?" Marianne asked.

"Yes. A month ago. Nothing I didn't know."

"Oh, come on."

"I'm Esther's best friend, remember?"

"What does that mean?"

"We read a lot. She's really smart, and she's into literature."

"Oh." Marianne contemplated this, before placing a hand on her sleeve, looking deeply into her eyes. "Consider The Book, though. Enter into marriage with God. It can be a beautiful thing, this union between two souls. Being human and beset with selfishness, it takes work. Hard work sometimes, but the blessings follow."

"I know, Marianne. I realize we're both older, set in our ways, so it will take sacrifice. I know."

Suddenly, Marianne drew Liz into a warm embrace, patted her back, and told her how happy she was for her. "I love you so much, Liz, and if ever anyone deserved this, it's you. I hope you will enjoy every moment of your wedding day."

"Thank you, Marianne. I love you, too. And thank you for your good advice."

They both turned to find Samuel pointing to the window.

"It's starting!" he yelped. "The snow!"

And sure enough, a fine whirl of snowflakes came down from the leaden skies, the temperature dropped, and the wind picked up as they watched.

"Well, here it comes. We'll have to make the best of it," Liz whispered.

The chores were done in record time, a quick supper was eaten by the light of the battery lamp, and darkness fell on the immaculate farm, the barn swept and cleaned, the immense shop laden with food and benches set for the hundreds of guests. In the house, there was a sense of having accomplished the Herculean task before them, and that anything was possible after today. Samuel kept up a newscaster's voice as he tracked the storm on his phone, which irritated Sylvia to no end. She barked at him to put that thing away, or she would.

Sarah and Suzanna, the little girls, as they were called, simply took all the excitement in stride, ran errands for Mam, giggled and crept around sneaking candy, lifting the corners of Tupperware cookie containers without replacing them tightly, which had Mam after them, scolding and lamenting the fact that the cookies would all be dried out. They weren't of course, but with the snow pouring from the sky, her anxiety level was on high alert, and that Samuel didn't help one bit.

Matthew knocked on the door of Liz's bedroom late that evening, took her in his arms, and told her he loved her.

"I mean it, Liz," he said against her still-damp hair. "I am not worthy of you now, and I never will be. I am a man blessed far beyond measure."

"Thank you, Matthew, for your love. I don't deserve you, either. We are blessed, both of us. Now you had better get to your bed, Mr. Zook, before I follow you there."

He laughed, and she clung to him for one delicious moment before softly closing her bedroom door, smiling to herself, remembering the soft texture of his good quality t-shirt, the strength of his back, his side.

"Lord, help me to be pleasing to him. Grant that our union will be blessed. I need You to stay by my side tomorrow, and for the rest of my life as Matthew's wife."

During the night, she awoke to hurry to her bedroom window to check on the snow's accumulation. She definitely had the jitters, thinking about buggies and vans sliding around in the snow. Would all the guests be able to arrive on time without a mishap? She sent a few prayers for the safety of each and every guest.

* * *

In the morning, the snow still swirled around buildings, but there was a small crease of pink in the West, loudly announced by Samuel, dressed in his new black suit, his white shirt buttoned to the top, his hair cut neatly, his eyes full of anticipation for the great day, a day of FUN.

Upstairs, Liz was applying a final spritz of hairspray on her neatly combed and rolled hair, before putting the black covering on her head, drawing the strings into a neat bow on her chest. She was pleased with the deep plum color against the white of the cape and apron. Matthew's sister Rachel arrived at that moment, her white cape and apron already pinned into place, but her two coverings carried in a box, a black one for the service and a white one for the afternoon and evening. She was dark haired, with Matthew's same green eyes, but had certainly not inherited his perfect features. However, there was a hidden grace, a shy sweetness about her, especially when she met Henry, dark-haired and handsome. Liz could not help but notice the way his gaze kept turning to Rachel. She sincerely hoped the decision to have him as *nāva sitza* would not cause problems for her best friend. With all the hustle and bustle of the last few weeks, Esther hadn't had the opportunity to tell Liz how she had begun to feel that Henry was, after all, not the right one for her.

Liz could only drink a few swallows of coffee, a crust of toast, before they made their way to the shop, shivering in the cold wind and flying snow, umbrellas held aloft. Sylvia ran ahead like a deer, heedless of any wind or snow. The skid loader flew around the farm like a frenzied workaholic, clearing a wide space for any vehicle or horse and buggy.

They lined up on the bench provided for them, greeted all the well wishers, relatives and friends, elderly folks to squalling babies. The aroma of food being prepared already permeated the huge area as a steady stream of guests filed in, shook hands, and greeted them with friendly smiles. Everyone agreed, the snow certainly did nothing to deter the usual anticipation of a wedding day, the pinnacle of Amish social gatherings.

As the congregation was being seated, the wind picked up, but after the first song was started, a steady brightening of the interior became evident. By the time the *hochzeita* (bride and groom) had filed solemnly to their appointed seats in the minister's row, there was an outpouring of sunlight through the large windows.

Matthew caught Liz's eye and blinked meaningfully without as much as a changed expression. She gave him the smallest of smiles. This was not a time to be caught smiling or laughing. This was a solemn occasion, a church service where God was certainly present, and so respect and sincerity were expected.

The sunshine flooding the room made their hearts even lighter, as they felt the blessing from the Lord.

And so, they were married, standing side by side in front of the kindly bishop who placed their hands in his and wished them the blessing of the God of Abraham, Isaac, and Jacob, after the solemn answer to the vows. It all seemed so sacred, so blessed, Liz could hardly breathe with the impact of being pronounced Matthew's wife. And that day, a desire to be all he thought she was rose in her, of which she never wavered. A true helpmeet, slow to anger and slow to condemnation, quick to praise and offer assistance, to consider his feelings as well as her own, in all ways she wanted to love and honor her husband.

As she was seated at the corner table (*ans eck*), she admired the lovely china, the beautiful knives and forks. Everything gleamed with the sunlight on new fallen snow. Pink hearts were scattered with silver ones for Valentine's Day.

The meal was like ambrosia, the *roascht* and mashed potatoes melting in her mouth, the fancy Jell-o and neatly prepared puddings and salads a treat to the palate. She could never remember a better meal or a happiness of this dimension. So many well wishers, so many hard-working individuals to make all this possible.

To see Matthew seated across the corner, resplendent in his black suit and white shirt, knowing he was her husband would have been all that was necessary. She realized that she would not have felt this same level of awe-inspiring sense of gratitude if she had not experienced the life sucking disappointment of Ray. It took her breath away to now be in this place of joy, hopes fulfilled, and the promise of a bright future.

She met his eyes, let the love and joy meet the love in his, before turning to speak to Henry, who was fully engaged in a conversation with Rachel. When they left the table to go to the gift-opening area, the first person to greet her was her closest friend, Esther. She hugged her, told her she looked beautiful.

"Your turn next, Esther," she said, smiling sincerely.

Esther waved a hand. "Hate to tell you, darling, but it's going nowhere. Sorry."

Liz stared at her. "Are you serious?"

"I didn't want to cause an upset before your wedding, but next week I'm going to have to tell him it's just not working. Liz, I have so much to tell you. Don't tell anyone else yet, but I'm moving to Mexico!"

"You're what?" Liz thought for a moment she was joking, but Esther sped on.

"To the Old Russian Mennonite Colony. I'm going to teach school there. I've been desperate to tell you." She grinned, full of excitement for her next adventure. "But this is your day. We can catch up later." She swung her hips as she walked away, smiling.

Only for a moment, Liz felt her joy drain away, replaced by a sadness that her best friend would be leaving and concern for Henry's inevitable heartbreak. She found Matthew and looped her arm through his for a brief second, a gesture of reassurance and gratitude. Then she caught sight of Henry deep in conversation with Rachel and thought perhaps this was all working out exactly the way it was meant to.

Annie came up to her, smiling as she lumbered toward her, favoring one hip. "I still can't believe I didn't know," she said, shaking her head. "I just had no idea you and Matthew were dating! Why wouldn't you tell me?" She pouted for a moment, then wrapped her in a big embrace, wishing her all the happiness in the world. Then she pulled back a bit and lowered her voice. "Did you hear about Priscilla?"

Liz shook her head, looking concerned.

"She ran off out west somewhere. Turns out she was seeing a married English man, except she didn't know he was married. Her parents found out and I guess there was quite a scene. Anyway, she up and left, bought herself a train ticket and took off." Annie shook her head and clucked her tongue, then hurried off to the dessert table.

Liz lifted a silent prayer for Priscilla, thinking perhaps getting away from her parents was the best thing she could have done, based on what Liz's brother had told her. She prayed God would protect her and draw her heart to himself. And then she trusted that God would fulfill His purpose in the young girl's life.

They moved to the gift corner where a group of friends sang in harmony, beautiful hymns printed on booklets made especially for this purpose. As the words of the hymns moved to her heart, Liz blinked back tears of joy, then reached for the first beautifully wrapped present, while Sylvia wrote every detail in a white composition book. So many gifts, such a wonderful array of useful items and beautiful things. A gas grill, a patio set, a wheelbarrow, a Stihl weedeater, a lawn mower, all the items a young couple would fully appreciate for a long time.

"It's just too much," she whispered to Matthew.

"It really is. I feel sort of guilty, actually."

Liz sent a quick prayer of thankfulness to swirl among the many voices still lifted in song. She caught her mother's eye, standing in the background, her mouth opened as she sang along, rejoicing, no doubt now that the sun had broken through and she had visible evidence of God being on her side after all.

Her heart swelled with love for her mother, bless her caring heart. Always *fa-sarking* (caring for), always wishing everyone the best, in her own way. Sometimes she simply cared too much and ended up making a mess of things, but that was just being a good mother.

And there was her father, tall and handsome, enjoying her wedding day to the fullest, exuberant with love and pride. Here was Liz, the one he'd pitied so deeply he could barely stand it, married to this fine young man, one who he could tell would treat Liz with every ounce of the love she deserved. *Gott isht good* (God is good).

Chapter Ten

AS FICKLE AS FEBRUARY CAN BE, THE DAY after the wedding was warm and sunny, water dripping from the eaves, snow melting into puddles everywhere.

Everyone was working hard, again, sweeping and scouring, wiping down tables and benches, carrying leftovers to the house to be divided among helpful relatives. The spirit of camaraderie still lingered, with well-meaning jokes exchanged, hearty guffaws of good humor, women fussing up a storm about the delicious food.

Never was a wedding perfect. Never. There were always the tense moments behind the scenes when the *roascht* was burnt or the gravy was lumpy and had to be put through a sieve, women cackling and fussing, placing unkind blame in the heat of the moment.

Mam was plain downright upset, though, finding the residue of burnt scalloped potatoes all over oven racks and bottoms of ovens.

"Who in the world would be so irresponsible?" She asked, a hand on one hip, wagging the arthritic forefinger.

Liz walked into the cooking area in time to find Aunt Malinda and Mam deciding on whom they would place the blame.

"That Barb can be a mess. Likely gawking around, not minding her business. Why this is an awful mess. Look at this. They could have remembered to turn the oven off. It's just so irresponsible."

"You know Katie isn't much better. She's a slop at home," her sister Malinda said, popping a cold meatball into her mouth.

"Ew. Malinda. How can you eat them?"

"They're good. Where's the ketchup?"

They spied Liz, her face radiant, wearing only a light sweater as the temperature rose.

"Here comes the bride," Malinda sang out.

"No, not the bride. The wife. *Die frau*," Liz corrected her.

"Laundry done?" her mother asked.

"Yep. All done. Now what?"

Mam checked Liz's face, the way mothers will do when occasion calls for silence, then smiled sincerely, relief flooding her voice as she said, "You can take this leftover lettuce in and bring the oven cleaner. These stoves were rented, and there's no way we can get them clean without it. Seriously, what were they thinking?"

Her sister wagged her head, clucked to let her know she too thought it was awful, before upending the ketchup bottle on a cold meatball and popping it into her mouth.

"Would you quit that?" Mam asked.

Malinda shook up and down, laughing, before eating another one.

They watched Liz carry the box of lettuce to the house, then looked at one another and winked simultaneously before turning back to the task at hand.

* * *

They moved to their newly purchased home the last week in February. It was a small Cape Cod under a huge maple tree, with overgrown yews flopping across the deep front porch, wide porch posts resting on sturdy brick pillars, and enough charm to captivate her heart for many years. The rooms were small, the kitchen cabinets a yellowing, greasy knotty pine, the shelves lined with torn contact paper.

They scrubbed and painted enough to get by, then moved in and set everything right. Their own furniture, their clothes hung in the cutest closets, the towels and bed sheets stored in little nooks and crannies made for that purpose. The smell of soap and deodorant, coffee brewing, a roast chicken in the oven—it all mingled together, making the house *their* home.

No matter that it was small and imperfect. No matter the kitchen floor was squares of broken black and white tile. This was their first cozy home, solid and serviceable, cozy in the harsh winds of February.

The only hardship was the visiting of relatives every weekend. *Yung kyot psucha* (newlywed visiting). A tradition from the old days, when a couple collected their wedding gifts while visiting the homes of the givers, a symbol of a returned kindness, an expected courtesy.

Every Saturday evening and every Sunday, they would go to the small barn, hitch up the horse to the carriage, and be off to visit yet another uncle or cousin or friend. Liz enjoyed it more than Matthew, who proclaimed the old tradition plain unhandy. Just when they could enjoy the peace and privacy of their own home, they were required to get on the road and visit everyone, every weekend.

"Not everyone," Liz would remind him.

"Almost."

Liz declared he was pouting, but Matthew laughed, said it was a small price to pay for being married to the love of his life.

Slushy mounds of melting snow lay by the road, the horse already slick with sweat as the March sun reminded them of spring's arrival. They spotted a few lambs in a barnyard, the anxious mothers stopping to watch as they went by.

"I can't wait for warmer weather," Matthew remarked.

"Me too. I'm really looking forward to putting all my energy into fixing up our place. Can you imagine what can be done?"

"Can't wait to work with you."

"Still," Liz mused. "I almost want to hang on to this winter."

"Why is that?"

"Oh, just because."

A comfortable silence hung between them as the spirited horse trotted briskly down the road. Liz drew the lap robe over her knees, snuggled close to her husband and thought how some things were simply too sacred to share with anyone. She thought of Mary, when the angel of the Lord spoke to her about being the mother of Jesus. She kept all these things and pondered them in her heart, the Bible said. And this was the very thing Liz wanted to keep, her own personal God-sent miracle.

She had been lifted from despair, from a sacrifice so great she could barely comprehend the depth of it. When she was sure he wanted Miriam and instead he asked Liz to marry him, would she ever think of that as anything but her own Christmas miracle?

She had become engaged when the snow swirled around the house, fell softly on the farm like a benediction, a blessing from God to remind her of His love. The joy of Christmas, the gift of the Baby Jesus all wrapped together with Matthew's love, filled her heart to overflowing, a constant reminder of the winter, the Christmas season of her personal miracle.

She sincerely hoped she would never take this lightly, would never forget to appreciate Matthew as her husband. When life handed them disappointments and trials, which were sure to come, she would always hope to overcome them with a grateful heart.

Christmas was always a favorite season, with the exuberance of children, the candles and greenery, the gaily wrapped packages displayed on a tablecloth-covered bureau in the living room. Cookie baking, the kitchen filled with the aroma of spices, chocolate, molasses, all of it blending to create the aura of the season. This year, there had been the wonder of the grandfather clock, the pendulum swinging rhythmically, every second ticking her own joyous heartbeat.

The snow and the cold following the engagement had been a time of joy as well. At the restaurant, when roads were treacherous and traffic slowed, there had been days when no one was busy, and still the joy lingered between cooking and serving the few customers who dared venture out on slippery roads.

The winter season had contained a lifetime of blessings, until Liz realized it was only those who tasted of the deepest disappointment who could be carried so high on wings of gratitude. And so her spirits soared, lost in thought as the buggy rumbled and swayed behind the steady clopping sound of the horse's hooves on macadam.

* * *

They arrived home late that evening, the buggy loaded down with useful items for the newlyweds. A hacksaw, a sledge hammer, a metal yard rake, and a fifty-dollar bill for Matthew. A set of stainless steel bowls, a potato masher, bath towels, and embroidered pillow cases.

Aus nā-us (embroidery) was an old, old skill, honored and upheld by the Amish community. In every home, there was *die goot schtup* (the good room) with an immaculate bed made up with pristine sheets, pillows encased in the embroidered pillowcases, a colorful design of vines and flowers or birds and butterflies. The pillowcase was often crocheted at the hem, an intricate shell design putting the final touch on *die schāney kupptziecha* (these nice pillowcases). After overnight guests spent a night beneath the handmade quilt and rested their heads on these pillowcases, everything was washed and ironed before being put on the bed for the next guest.

Mommy Esh had presented them to Liz with so much pride, saying she knew they were outdated, but she so enjoyed making them for her, and Liz hugged her in gratitude, said she would surely use them in honor of her, which left Mommy Esh wiping away a discrete tear after they left.

Die yung kyate. What a blessing, these couples starting out together, the builders of the church, the helpers to unite them all. Mommy Esh thought fondly of her own newlywed visiting, the times when folks still had *die schtup* (the room). This room was like the parlor of old, kept closed off to the normal household activities, opened only upon the arrival of special guests—especially the honored newlyweds. This room had woven carpets, in long, narrow strips,

laid together to resemble wall to wall carpeting. There
were wood rocking chairs with colorful embroidered
pillows. Everyone prized the art of fine needlework,
and no house was complete without it. There would
be a bureau, solid oak and varnished to a high gloss,
with an embroidered dresser scarf gracing the top.
In the middle, the water set would take up most of
the space, the pitcher and six glasses presented to the
bride before the wedding then placed on the bureau
for twenty or thirty years or more. The sideboard
would often hold a berry set, a bowl with small ones
nestled in it, and other glassware too pretty to use. A
family record would always be hung on the wall, with
other framed needlework or a pretty calendar.

And Mommy Fsh thought fondly of all these
details, in an era that no longer existed, or rarely.
But, she reasoned, you had to go with the times, you
couldn't sit around and get old and sour, now could
you? And wasn't it something how the young people still gave themselves up to go visiting among the
community, in spite of the lost art of the needlework?
Oh, she was certainly grateful.

Liz ran her fingers over the delicate embroidery, a smile forming as she shook her head.

"Matthew, look at this. Endless hours of work, to adorn pillowcases. Can you imagine? Guests who sleep in this bed, with the ends of the pillowcase barely visible in the light of a smelly old kerosene lamp. Seriously."

"Oh, but her heart is happy, knowing she has done everything her mother taught her. She has fulfilled her housekeeping skills valued so highly among us to this day," he said, coming to stand beside her at the kitchen table.

"I know. But isn't it senseless?"

"No, no. Not to Mommy. She loves the old way."

Suddenly Liz turned to Matthew and told him she was going to have a *goot schtup*. Yes. She would use white sheets, these embroidered pillowcases, a colorful handmade quilt, and put it on her parents' old sleigh bed. She would paper the walls, hang a pretty calendar, put the green blinds in the window.

Matthew smiled, then took her gently into his arms, said he was so proud of her, honoring his grandmother like that. And she smiled up into his eyes and said she would like to honor her with another old tradition, and when he raised his eyebrows in question, she told him very seriously she would love to have at least ten children.

Matthew held his precious wife close, and she smiled with her cheek on his shirtfront. She felt God smiling down on them, she felt His blessing, and thought you never knew what wondrous gifts would flow from a surprise Christmas engagement.

THE END

Other Books by Linda Byler

LIZZIE SEARCHES FOR LOVE SERIES

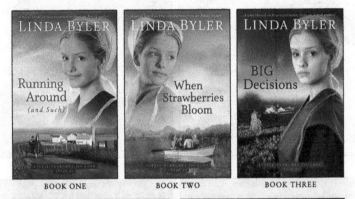

BOOK ONE   BOOK TWO   BOOK THREE

TRILOGY   COOKBOOK

Sadie's Montana Series

BOOK ONE

BOOK TWO

BOOK THREE

TRILOGY

LANCASTER BURNING SERIES

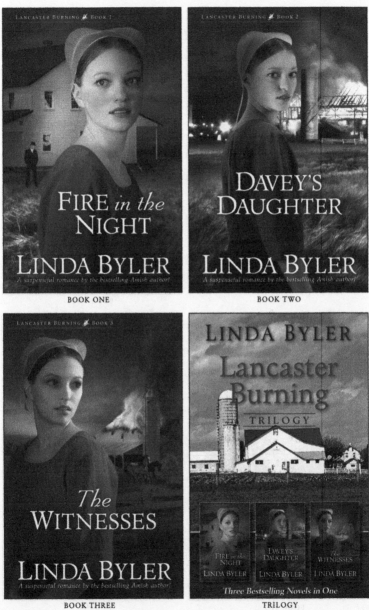

LANCASTER BURNING ✦ BOOK 1

FIRE *in the*
NIGHT

LINDA BYLER

A suspenseful romance by the bestselling Amish author!

BOOK ONE

LANCASTER BURNING ✦ BOOK 2

DAVEY'S
DAUGHTER

LINDA BYLER

A suspenseful romance by the bestselling Amish author!

BOOK TWO

LANCASTER BURNING ✦ BOOK 3

The
WITNESSES

LINDA BYLER

A suspenseful romance by the bestselling Amish author!

BOOK THREE

LINDA BYLER
Lancaster
Burning
TRILOGY

FIRE *in the* NIGHT
LINDA BYLER

DAVEY'S DAUGHTER
LINDA BYLER

The WITNESSES
LINDA BYLER

Three Bestselling Novels in One

TRILOGY

BOOK ONE

BOOK TWO

BOOK THREE

TRILOGY

BOOK ONE

BOOK TWO

BOOK THREE

TRILOGY

THE LONG ROAD HOME

BOOK ONE

COMING SOON

BOOK TWO

COMING SOON

BOOK THREE

CHRISTMAS COLLECTIONS

AMISH CHRISTMAS ROMANCE COLLECTION   AMISH ROMANCE AT CHRISTMASTIME

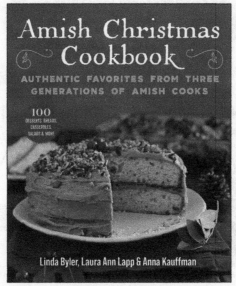

AMISH CHRISTMAS COOKBOOK

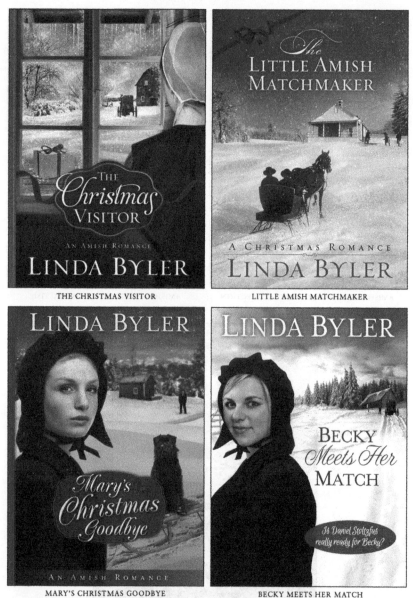

THE CHRISTMAS VISITOR

LITTLE AMISH MATCHMAKER

MARY'S CHRISTMAS GOODBYE

BECKY MEETS HER MATCH

A DOG FOR CHRISTMAS

A HORSE FOR ELSIE

THE MORE THE MERRIER

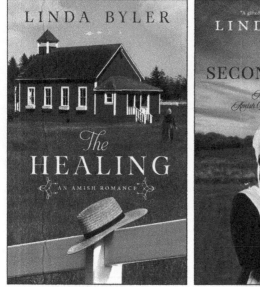

THE HEALING

A SECOND CHANCE

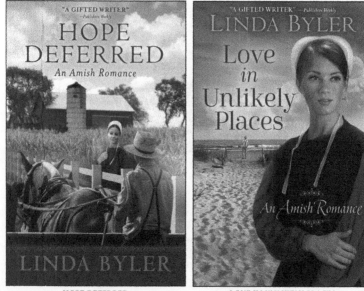

HOPE DEFERRED

LOVE IN UNLIKELY PLACES

BOOK ONE

BOOK TWO

BOOK THREE

About the Author

LINDA BYLER WAS RAISED IN AN AMISH FAMILY and is an active member of the Amish church today. Growing up, Linda loved to read and write. In fact, she still does. Linda is well-known within the Amish community as a columnist for a weekly Amish newspaper. She writes all her novels by hand in notebooks.

Linda is the author of many novels including several series, all set among the Amish communities of North America: Lizzie Searches for Love, Sadie's Montana, Lancaster Burning, Hester's Hunt for Home, The Dakota Series, The Long Road Home, and the Buggy Spoke Series for younger readers. Linda has also written a number of Christmas romances set among the Amish: *Mary's Christmas Goodbye*, *The Christmas Visitor*, *The Little Amish Matchmaker*, *Becky Meets Her Match*, *A Dog for Christmas*, *A Horse for Elsie*, and *The More the Merrier*. Linda has coauthored *Lizzie's Amish Cookbook: Favorite Recipes from Three Generations of Amish Cooks!* and *Amish Christmas Cookbook*.